Dear Reader,

We're a mother-daughter writing team (Barbara is the mother, and Pam is the daughter) and have been working together for more than twenty years. The process of collaboration is very gratifying.

In *Winds of Change,* we once again have the opportunity to visit the charming town of Marble Cove to bring to life the stories of a wonderful group of women. Returning to this Maine locale—and to Diane, Margaret, Beverly and Shelley—is like reuniting with friends.

In this story, the theme of change and how the women react to the upheaval in their lives runs strong. Throughout our own lives, both of us have had to make life-transforming decisions. We have been blessed to be able to lean on family, friends and faith to make sometimes difficult choices.

When an overwhelmed Shelley finds herself with sudden extra help, she must learn to decide if it's a blessing or a hindrance. But she has no trouble relying on her good friends as they continue to try to unravel the mystery surrounding the venerable Old First Church.

We hope you enjoy your time spent in Marble Cove with these four special friends as much as we do.

All the best!
Pam Hanson & Barbara Andrews

WINDS OF CHANGE

MIRACLES *of*
MARBLE COVE

WINDS OF CHANGE

PAM HANSON &
BARBARA ANDREWS

New York, New York

Miracles of Marble Cove is a trademark of Guideposts.

Published by Guideposts Books & Inspirational Media
110 William Street
New York, NY 10038
Guideposts.org

Acknowledgments

Every attempt has been made to credit the sources of copyrighted material
used in this book. If any such acknowledgment has been inadvertently
omitted or miscredited, receipt of such information would be appreciated.

"From the Guideposts Archive" originally appeared as "His Mysterious
Ways" by Ann-Marie Walker in *Guideposts* magazine. Copyright © 2004
by Guideposts. All rights reserved.

Cover and interior design by Müllerhaus
Cover photo by iStock
Cover background by Jeremy Charles
Typeset by Aptara

Printed and bound in the United States of America
10 9 8 7 6 5 4

CHAPTER ONE

S helley Bauer laid aside the scoop she was using to drop cookie dough on a baking sheet and picked up the ringing phone.

"Lighthouse Sweet Shoppe," she said in a cheerful voice. She was still thrilled by hearing the name she'd given her baking business. "How may I help you?"

"Do you bake cakes?" an elderly voice asked.

"Yes, we certainly do," she said, smiling at the use of the plural since she was the owner, manager, and baker, all rolled up into one.

"I'm having a little celebration for Herbert—that's my husband. He'll be ninety next week, and he's always loved my chocolate cake. It's getting hard for me to bake, so I wonder, can you make a homemade birthday cake? He doesn't like powdered sugar frosting. It has to have the fluffy kind you make with egg whites."

"That's no problem," Shelley said, propping up the phone on her shoulder so she could write the customer's information on her order pad. "When will you need it?"

"Four days from now on Wednesday, that's the sixth of March. I'm afraid I can't pick it up. Can you deliver?"

"Do you live in Marble Cove?" Shelley asked. The gray sky outside her big windows warned of bad weather to come, and she really didn't want to drive too far from town.

"Oh yes, we're on Water Street about two blocks from the ocean." It was just one street over. "We live on the lower floor and rent out the upper, so be sure to ring the bell by the door with the oval glass."

Shelley patiently took down the client's information, a slow process since the woman embellished all the details with reminiscences of past birthdays. She vaguely remembered seeing the elderly couple out for walks in the neighborhood, but then, she'd lived in the small Maine town since her marriage and pretty much knew most of the residents by sight, if not by name. In the summer, it was different. Summer people and tourists flooded the town, more than doubling the population.

"Thank you for your order," she said to conclude the conversation.

Still smiling, Shelley hung the slip on the small board with hooks her husband Dan had made to help her keep track of what she had to bake. There were already three other orders for Wednesday, and she tried to work out a schedule in her mind. The way it looked, she was going to be short on sleep over the next few days.

When she'd first thought of starting a cookie business, she'd never dreamed of expanding into all kinds of baking. She thanked the Lord every day for the opportunity to show what she could do, and also for the beautiful new kitchen her father-in-law and husband had added to the back of their bungalow-style house—even if it did smell slightly of paint. Now she had commercial-grade stainless steel appliances, a huge pantry, granite counters, and a marble-topped island for rolling pastry. Even better, light flooded in through large windows and the French doors. She had a wonderful view of the backyard, where her four-year-old son Aiden could sometimes wander in and out with his dog when the weather was fine, and Shelley could work in the kitchen.

"Look who's up," Dan said, walking into the kitchen with a sleepy-eyed Emma in his arms and Prize, their son's beagle/cocker spaniel, dogging his heels.

Shelley reached out her arms and took her daughter, tickling her nose against the fine blonde hair on Emma's head. She was still wearing her pink flannel pajamas with footies, and Shelley would've loved to sit and cuddle her until she was fully awake. Unfortunately, she only had time for a quick hug. She put Emma in the corner playpen, a necessity when Shelley had hot ovens, so she'd stay out of trouble for a few minutes until her breakfast was ready.

"Out you go, Prize," Dan said, letting the dog into the fenced backyard still covered with gray snow piles turned to ice in the melting/freezing weather of late winter. "Not very inviting out there," he said to Shelley.

"No, but bad weather isn't hurting business." She glanced at Emma, glad to see her happily playing with a sock doll her grandmother had made. "I've had an order already this morning. Will you be able to deliver a cake Wednesday on Water Street?"

Since Dan had been laid off from his job at the docks, she tried hard not to assume he was available for any chore she needed done. He was extremely handy and good at picking up odd jobs, but at this time of year not even Margaret had work for him. She hoped her friend would have more art to be framed for the Shearwater Gallery soon, but for now her handsome young husband was mainly responsible for their two children.

"Remind me the night before," he said, stooping to watch his daughter at play. "Do you want me to get her breakfast?"

"I'll do it," she said, torn between wanting to be with her youngest and needing to finish the cookies she was making for the Cove, the coffee shop that was still her biggest customer.

"I'll run some errands, then," Dan said, standing and giving Shelley a quick kiss. "Is Adelaide coming today?"

Margaret's daughter Adelaide was a blessing to the Bauer family. Although she had Down syndrome, at age twenty-five she functioned well as a playmate and sitter for Aiden and Emma, not to mention helping out in the kitchen from time to time. Her helpful nature and sweet spirit brought out the best in the children, and she was always welcome in their home. Now that Shelley had to spend so much time building her business, she didn't know how she'd get along without her help.

"She goes to the community center this morning, but she's coming this afternoon. She can entertain Aiden and Emma after their naps."

Shelley watched her tall, sandy-haired husband leave, but she didn't have time to worry about his lost job. Before she could start Emma's breakfast, the phone rang again.

"Lighthouse Sweet Shoppe," she said automatically.

"You sound so professional," Diane Spencer said.

Shelley smiled at the sound of her friend's voice. She really didn't have time to chat on the phone, but hearing from her neighbor made her day a little brighter.

Diane was relatively new to Marble Cove, but their friendship had come to mean a great deal to Shelley. Diane was in her midfifties, a widow and a writer whose first mystery had been accepted by a publisher. In spite of the differences in their ages and occupations, Shelley immensely enjoyed knowing her and would have loved to have a long chat on the phone. Unfortunately, there were too many demands on her time at the moment.

"I guess you could say business is booming," Shelley said. "I'm getting orders from people I don't even know, and that's saying a lot in Marble Cove."

"Are the kiddos up?"

"Emma is. She's in her playpen waiting for breakfast, but Aiden is still sleeping. Whoops, here he is now," Shelley said, smiling at her four-year-old as he shuffled into the kitchen in his footed PJs. "Good morning, sleepyhead."

"I can't find my red hoodie," Aiden said, stopping to see what his sister was up to in the playpen.

"It's in the laundry. I haven't had a chance to wash it. Sorry, Diane, I didn't mean to interrupt our conversation."

"Hey, kids come first. When my two were little, I didn't even try to work as much as you do. I have a thought. How about I come over and cook them breakfast?"

"I don't want you to stop writing on my account," Shelley said, much as she welcomed her friend's offer.

"I haven't even sat down at my computer in two days. I can't seem to get rolling on this second book, even though I have an editor waiting for the manuscript. I'd love to help with Emma and Aiden for a little while."

"I would so appreciate it," Shelley said, pushing back a lock of long blonde hair escaping from her ponytail. "I'm in the middle of a cookie order for the Cove. I should've asked Dan to stay, but he gets so restless if he doesn't get out from time to time."

"Any job prospects?"

Shelley knew Diane was asking out of concern.

"Afraid not. I pray every day something will come up, but March is an awful month for job hunting around here."

"I'm sure he'll find something soon. Dan is handy at so many things. Well, I'll put out some dog food for Rocky and come over. It looks so dreary out there, he'll have to wait until this afternoon for his walk. See you soon!"

"Mama, I need my red hoodie," Aiden said as soon as Shelley hung up, quickly losing interest in the sock doll he'd snatched from his sister.

"Honey, I know it's your favorite, but it has to be washed. Give the doll back to Emma. Diane is coming over. Why don't you find something else to wear before she gets here?"

"Can I wear the new shirt Grandma gave me?"

"No, that's for Sunday school."

"I don't have anything to wear!" he protested indignantly.

"Look in your drawers. I'm sure you'll find something. I think your yellow shirt with the bear is clean."

"Jeremy said it's a baby shirt."

"Jeremy is wrong. Bears are big strong animals. Put on your yellow shirt, and you can show me how fierce bears are."

Aiden grumbled but stomped off to his bedroom to get dressed. Why did simple things like keeping the kids clothed seem so complicated these days? She'd never given the laundry much thought until she got so busy with her business.

Emma started squealing and jumping up and down, her way of protesting imprisonment in the playpen. She was too active to be happy there for more than a few minutes. Shelley went to the new dining area and carried the high chair out to the kitchen. Emma squirmed as Shelley tried to seat her daughter in it, wiggling more as she tied on a bib although the front of her nightclothes was already damp. She was teething hard and soaking through everything she wore, necessitating frequent changes. Shelley knew how much laundry was stacked up waiting to be washed, but with luck both kids could go another day. She just didn't have time today, and Dan was never keen to tackle that job.

"Hello, I'm here," Diane called out as she opened the front door.

"Come on in," Shelley said, keeping one eye on Emma while she went to welcome her friend.

"Just let me take off my Bogs and coat," Diane said. "You can go back to what you were doing."

Even early in the morning, Diane was good-humored and ready to be helpful. She was tall and thin with shoulder-length brown hair that never looked scruffy or windblown. Like Shelley, she had blue eyes, but hers had a memorable twinkle, and at the same time radiated kindness and concern for others. She came into the kitchen wearing jeans, a caramel colored suede shirt and the thick wool socks she always wore under her waterproof hiking boots.

"Well, good morning, Emma," she said, bringing a smile to the toddler's face. "What a funny bunny you have there."

Emma looked down at her bib and repeated the word as though seeing the cartoon character for the first time. Diane adored both Bauer children and had confessed her eagerness to have a grandchild someday, although neither of her grown children had given her much hope yet.

"I'm sorry to hear your book isn't going well," Shelley said as she put on water for the children's hot cereal.

"It's not going at all, sad to say," Diane admitted. "I just can't seem to wrap my mind around a fictional mystery when we have a real puzzle right here in Marble Cove."

"Hi, Diane," Aiden said, returning to the kitchen dressed in faded purple sweatpants and a grayish white T-shirt long ago forgotten in a corner of his drawer. He'd managed to stuff his feet into worn-out fuzzy dog-head slippers his mother had tried to throw out at least three times.

"*Miss* Diane," Shelley corrected automatically, deciding to worry about a warmer shirt after the cookies were baked. The kitchen was warm enough for him to run around in his underwear when she was baking. "I'll have some oatmeal for you in a minute."

"I hate oatmeal."

Emma slapped her tray with both hands, seemingly in agreement.

"You like it." Shelley was hard put to conceal her frustration. Her son's latest ploy for attention was to "hate" everything she fixed for meals.

"You've probably never played the oatmeal game," Diane said with a mischievous smile.

"What's that?" Aiden sounded interested but skeptical. He wasn't as easy to woo as he'd once been.

"I'll show you when it's ready," she promised.

After she served up the oatmeal, poured orange juice, and cut the crust off toast triangles, Shelley returned to her baking, putting chocolate chip cookies in the oven and dropping scoops of dough on another pan while Diane played a word game with Aiden. He was having so much fun he forgot about hating oatmeal and asked for a second helping. Emma was a novice at feeding herself, but she was occupied smearing cereal on her face, hands, and the tray. Some even made it to her mouth.

When the cookies on the pan were done, Shelley transferred them to a cooling rack and put more into her big commercial-size oven. It was wonderful to be able to fit two large baking sheets on a rack compared to the single smaller one she could do in her old one.

"Smells wonderful," Diane said. "It's a treat to sit in your kitchen when you're baking."

"Which is most of the time lately," Shelley said.

"It's wonderful your business has taken off so well."

"Yes, I thank the Lord every time I start baking. It's going better than I ever dreamed possible."

"I'm so happy for you, but you do look tired. Is there anything I can do to help?"

"Just being my friend is wonderful help."

"Mama, may I have a cookie?" Aiden asked when he'd finished his breakfast.

"Honey, they're much too hot. Anyway, we don't have dessert for breakfast. I'll save one for you to have after lunch."

"But, Mama, I said 'May I!'"

Diane chuckled.

"Maybe later, Aiden," Shelley said.

"Emma doesn't get cookies," Aiden told Diane with big-brother satisfaction.

"Emma gets her own special cookie," his mother reminded him.

"She gets a baby cookie," he told Diane. "Can I watch cartoons?"

Shelley hated using the TV to occupy her children, but she was feeling a bit desperate this morning.

"If you play nicely with Emma until I'm through with the cookies, you may watch a half hour."

"She doesn't play good," he complained on his way out of the kitchen.

Diane used a warm washcloth to clean Emma's face and freed her to toddle after her brother.

"They get cuter every day," Diane declared.

Prize was scratching to come inside. Shelley was surprised she'd stayed out so long, but then, her name was short for Surprise, a name well suited to her personality.

Diane let her in and took the children's dishes to the sink, rinsing them before putting them in the dishwasher.

"You don't have to do that," Shelley protested.

"No problem. How are you doing on the Internet? I looked up your Web site, and I was tempted to order something myself. The granola carrot cookies are new, aren't they?"

"Yes, I found the recipe in an old book and adjusted it for easier packing and shipping. I've only had a few orders so far, but the feedback has been great. Most of my sales are still local."

"You must be baking from morning to night."

"Pretty much so. Cookies are easy, but I've branched out into all kinds of baked goods except bread. A caterer and an out-of-town restaurant have placed some orders too. The restaurant features a dessert cart, and they were impressed by the number of people who selected my chocolate cheesecake."

"Wow! I'm beginning to feel like a slacker. You're filling orders right and left, and I can't even produce a chapter."

"Don't feel that way. Writing a book is a whole lot harder than baking. You can't measure out a cup of mystery and two tablespoons of suspense."

"Would that I could! Ever since Beverly and I discovered the hidden bell tower at Old First Church, my mind hasn't been at ease. I've read and tried to decipher the letters we found in Jeremiah Thorpe's trunk." Diane's face took on a faraway look. "Imagine how hard it was to communicate in the eighteenth century. People saved letters back in those days. They were so precious that Evangeline must have brought them with her on her journey to America."

"Have you learned anything else by rereading them?"

"Not really. The writing is faded and hard to make out, but the reference to a hidden treasure is pretty clear."

"It gives me shivers to think that maybe pirates left treasure here," Shelley said. "I wonder what happened to them. If their ship wrecked, how was the treasure saved?"

"The possibilities are certainly exciting," Diane said. "I'd like to go over the letters with Reverend Locke, but he wasn't at all happy when we found the lost bell tower. I have a feeling he'd just toss the letters aside for another hundred years if he knew about them. He's only interested in the here and now, especially renovations for the church."

"It's an odd way for him to act, considering he's the minister at Old First," Shelley said.

"I've been wondering whether Reverend Locke already knows something about Jeremiah Thorpe's lost treasure," Diane speculated. "Maybe he wants to keep its existence a secret."

"That could explain why he was so upset when you and Beverly found the hidden tower," Shelley said, pausing from her work to ponder this new possibility.

"If he does know, he's not going to talk to any of us about it," Diane said regretfully. "Someday we'll have to return the letters to the church, though I don't know how we'll manage that, if Reverend Locke doesn't want us to. But meanwhile, there are still parts we haven't been able to read. There's always the possibility of finding clues to the location of the treasure."

"Mama!" Aiden interrupted their conversation with a loud shout. "Emma has my car!"

The timer on the stove shrilled insistently, and Shelley rushed to check the cookies. She took the pans out as quickly as possible and hurried to the front room to settle the squabble.

"I'm sorry," Diane said with a good-natured laugh. "This probably isn't the best time for my visit. I think I'll brave the March winds and take Rocky for his walk. Wish me luck not falling on slippery pavement."

"Be careful!" Shelley warned. "And thanks for coming over. I really needed to hear a little adult conversation."

She watched Diane leave, wondering if her friend would be able to make more progress in deciphering Jeremiah Thorpe's letters. She didn't know much about the founder of the lighthouse, but there seemed to be more mysteries in Marble Cove than in the mystery Diane would soon have published.

CHAPTER TWO

Margaret Hoskins felt a bit lazy driving her daughter Adelaide the short distance to Shelley's house instead of walking, but she wasn't feeling her best today. In fact, she hadn't had her usual zip all winter since the big scare about her health the month before. Fortunately, she hadn't had a heart attack, but she was taking the wake-up call seriously now.

The gloomy gray day matched her mood, but she was trying to focus on the promise of spring. Next to painting and running her art gallery, her favorite activity was gardening. She was already planning how to make her garden as lovely as always and still have time to care for it. Even now, the seed catalogs were stacked up waiting for her to make selections.

"Gordon is sick," Adelaide said, her voice full of concern for a little boy she knew from volunteering at the community day care center.

"That's a shame. Did he come to day care today?" Margaret was always concerned her daughter might be exposed to a virus, but it was so important for her to have contact with others. It was so easy for a Down syndrome young adult to become isolated, and she was beginning to feel that she and her husband Allan had only begun to recognize her potential and all the ways Adelaide could contribute to the community.

"No, he went to the doctor. Do you think he'll get a shot?" Adelaide asked.

"Only if he needs one," Margaret said. "Maybe he'll get some medicine to make him better."

Margaret worried about what would happen to Adelaide after she and Allan passed away. She was working hard to make her art gallery a success, hoping to add a significant amount to the trust fund she and Allan had set up for their daughter. And she hoped the royalties she would receive from her Lighting the Way greeting cards would continue to help support Adelaide for many years to come.

Of course, she wanted to be in Adelaide's life as long as possible, which meant she had to pay more attention to her own health. Besides monitoring her diet and taking supplements, she was seriously considering some kind of exercise program, as her doctor had suggested. Earlier she had decided to take one of the exercise classes the community center offered, but now she was having second thoughts about panting and sweating in a whole roomful of people.

Most of the winter had been spent getting ready for the summer rush at her art gallery. Her paintings had sold well to the summer crowd last year, and her lighthouse scenes were doing well in the greeting card line. She was hard-pressed to get enough paintings done for the coming season, but it was time to get serious about a sensible exercise program. Between the cold Maine winter and the time she spent painting, Margaret knew she had not been as active as she should be.

"Aiden got a new toy car," Adelaide told her, eagerly looking forward to her time with the Bauer children as she always did. "It's blue."

"That's nice, dear," Margaret answered absentmindedly, still wondering what a woman in her late sixties could do for exercise in the winter. She loved to swim in the sea, but Maine had a very short season for enjoying the ocean. And the weather and icy conditions made regular walking too unpredictable.

"Maybe Shelley will give me a cookie," her daughter speculated.

"Not today, Adelaide. You had ice cream for lunch. That's enough sweets for today."

"All right, Mom," Adelaide agreed. "No cookies today."

Margaret was thankful for her daughter's cooperative nature. Although she was short and stocky, she knew it was a bad thing to eat poorly and gain weight. She was conscious of her appearance and always kept her honey-colored shoulder-length hair brushed into soft waves. She took care in selecting what to wear every day and had a good idea of what was appropriate.

Activities at the community center and helping with Shelley's children gave focus to Adelaide's days, and she loved doing things for others, especially little ones.

Margaret and Allan had almost given up on having a child when they were blessed with their daughter twenty-five years ago. They never stopped marveling at how much she enriched their lives and brought them closer together.

"I had ice cream already," Adelaide repeated.

"Yes, tell that to Shelley if she offers you a cookie."

Margaret pulled into her friend's driveway and walked to the front door holding Adelaide's hand as much for her own support as her daughter's. She shivered a little in the biting March wind and thought of how nice it would be to pack away her bright blue down-filled coat until next fall. It was wonderful for keeping warm in the harsh winters, but it did nothing for her short stature and rounded contours. Worse, the hood made her short gray hair hug her head like a helmet.

Shelley met them at the door with flushed pink cheeks and strands of hair slipping from her blonde ponytail. Margaret's nose immediately caught the wonderful aroma of chocolate and cinnamon, a sure sign the younger woman had been hard at work baking.

"I'm so happy to see you, Adelaide," she said, giving her helper a little hug. "I couldn't possibly fill all my orders today without your help."

"She's eager to play with the children," Margaret said.

"Aiden is in his room," Shelley said. "Why don't you go say hello to him, Adelaide? And you can peek in on Emma. I wouldn't be surprised if she's waking up from her nap by now."

"Well, I'll leave you to your baking," Margaret said, backing off the rubber mat Shelley kept by the front door in winter.

"Wait. There's something I wanted to ask you," Shelley said when Adelaide was out of hearing. "I appreciate Adelaide's help so much, especially now that my business is taking off. Aiden and Emma adore her, and she's great at keeping them occupied."

"She really looks forward to being with your children," Margaret said, hoping Shelley wasn't going to tell her she'd made other arrangements for the children's care.

"Dan and I wondered whether it would be all right if we pay Adelaide for babysitting. I know you've refused before, but it only seems fair since she is such a big help."

"I don't know. She gets as much out of being here as you do in having her."

"Since I have so much baking to do, I don't feel right taking advantage of her. She is so good with the children."

"Tell you what. I'll talk it over with Allan. We've been encouraging her to be more independent. She could use the earnings to practice handling money. She was introduced to it in a life skills class, but she's never had much of a chance to put what she learned in action. If he agrees, you could give her a small amount. It certainly shouldn't be very much," Margaret said.

"Good. You can let me know," Shelley said.

"I think Allan will go along with it as long as you don't give her too much, maybe a few dollars each time she comes.

I'll talk to him about it right away. The more I think about it, the more I think it would be good for Adelaide to learn her babysitting has value."

"It certainly is valuable to me."

"I'd better get going," Margaret said. "When do you want me to pick her up?"

"She can stay as long as you like. She has amazing patience with my kids."

"How about five o'clock?"

"Great. I should have today's baking under control by then."

Margaret made stops at the bank and the market after leaving Shelley's house, stocking up on groceries for the next few days. She was carrying several bags into the house when she had an uncomfortable sensation in her chest. She put her load on the kitchen counter and took a few deep breaths.

Her doctor had assured her the occasional pains were caused by low potassium. She reached up to the high shelf where they still kept medicines away from Adelaide, although in all fairness, Margaret realized, she was good about not getting into things she shouldn't. After taking a couple of potassium pills, she felt better, although she knew they really couldn't have worked that fast.

Maybe she hadn't been paying attention to her diet as well as she should. Allan fixed most of their meals, and he was conscientious about what they ate. Maybe she just hadn't been eating enough bananas and apricots. Either way, she had to do more to keep in shape. As Allan liked to say, getting old wasn't for sissies.

As she put away the groceries, Margaret again tried to think of exercises congenial to a woman her age. The answer came to her as she was reaching up to put a bottle of vinegar on the high shelf over the stove. Reaching made her feel worse, but she thought of one person who could give her practical advice on getting into better shape: Beverly Wheeland-Parker.

Margaret didn't want to interrupt Beverly's work at home, knowing how frustrating it could be for her to be distracted when she was trying to complete a painting and too many people called or came over. She looked at the clock and decided to leave a phone message for Beverly. She was known to turn off her cell phone when she was in the middle of something.

Beverly is as fit as a person can be, Margaret thought, going to the phone and dialing her number.

There was no answer, and Margaret left a message for Beverly to call back when she had time. She definitely wanted her advice on exercise. She was younger than Margaret, still in her early forties, and she was a model of fitness. She ran in all kinds of weather, and regularly jogged along the beach as far as the lighthouse when she could.

If anyone knew good ways to keep in shape, it was Beverly. Maybe she had some advice that would work for a woman in her late sixties.

CHAPTER THREE

I don't feel good!" Aiden sat on his bed with one shoe on and one shoe off, sniffing dramatically.

Shelley looked with distress at her son. His big blue eyes were watery, and freckles stood out on his pale face. His nose did seem a little runny. She had to admit he didn't look his usual perky self.

"Emma's ready to go," Dan said, coming into the room carrying his daughter.

"He's not feeling well," Shelley said. "Maybe a cold?"

"Not in the mood for church this morning?" Dan asked a bit skeptically as Emma squirmed to get down.

"No, Daddy!" Aiden cried, the tears beginning to flow.

Shelley and Dan looked at each other and came to a silent understanding.

"I know you like your Sunday school class, but maybe you'd better stay home this morning." Dan turned to Shelley and volunteered to stay home with their son.

"Thanks, I appreciate it."

"I know how much church means to you. While I'm at it, you might as well leave Emma home too."

"Good idea. I know her nose is runny from teething, but the women in the nursery might think she has a cold."

She touched Aiden's forehead, but he didn't seem to have a fever.

"You can take some of that grape-flavored medicine," she said to her son.

"I'll take care of it," Dan assured her.

With the decision made, Shelley hurried to be on time for her adult Sunday school class. She loved the spiritual boost that came from regularly attending Light the Way Chapel. The church had a dynamic pastor and many young families, and she appreciated the Christian fellowship.

She checked herself in the bedroom mirror, straightening the pink lamb's wool sweater Dan had given her two years ago for Christmas. She'd opted to wear her navy slacks because cold March winds were howling around the house, and she could hear tree branches groaning from the force.

"Better wear your heavy coat," Dan said, going to the door with Emma toddling beside him. "This rain may turn to snow later on."

Shelley had already taken her rain slicker from the hanger, but Dan was probably right. He'd worked outside on the docks before he was laid off, and he had a keen instinct for weather.

"I hope Aiden isn't too sick," she said, slipping into her warmly lined nylon jacket.

"We'll hope it's blue flu," he said with a smile. "I remember developing mysterious ills when I was a kid and didn't want to go somewhere."

"He loves Sunday school," Shelley insisted.

"He did last week, but he's four, Shell. No telling what goes on in his head. I quit school in the first grade—refused to go into the classroom because some kid made a nasty remark. I sat out in the hall until my mom came and convinced me there was no choice."

"You never told me that!" she said with a laugh.

"School wasn't my thing, much to my parents' disappointment," he said. "But you'd better leave so you don't have to drive fast."

Shelley didn't think she'd get into trouble on the short ride to the chapel, but Dan's concern made her feel cherished.

The church parking lot was nearly full, a testament to the faithfulness of the congregation for coming out on what was turning into really unpleasant weather. The wind whipped at Shelley's cheeks and blew her hair every which way as she hurried into the building. By the time she hung up her jacket and ducked into the restroom to run a comb through her tangled blonde hair, she just made it to the adult class before the opening prayer.

The class was studying the book of Mark, and Shelley listened as Mrs. Horning read the verses. The disciples wanted Jesus to tell them who was greatest among them.

She tried to listen and learn, but her lids were heavy and her attention wandered. Somehow she had to get more sleep, but how could she turn down orders when her family needed the income?

When the class was over, Shelley wanted to splash some cold water on her face before the service began, but Mrs. Horning called out to her.

"Shelley, has anyone asked you about the women's retreat next weekend? We'll be going to the same conference center as last year. Whenever I've gone, it's been very rewarding."

Sondra Horning was past president of the congregation and one of the most active members, donating her time without reservation. She was also a friendly, outgoing person who made others feel good about themselves. Graying curls hugged her head, and she tended to wear some shade of blue most of the time. The little round lenses in her glasses gave her an owlish appearance, but her smile was friendly and warm.

"I'm afraid I can't possibly go," Shelley said, feeling a bit disappointed because Sondra was a person who was hard to turn down. "I've been terribly busy with my baking business and, of course, my children."

"I fully understand," Sondra said. "I was going to ask you something else. We have to take our own food to the camp. All the ladies loved the cookies you made for the last potluck. Would you mind making a few dozen for the retreat? You can bring them to the church any time before noon on Friday."

Shelley wanted to say no. At some point—soon, she realized—she'd have to put her foot down about baking for free. But how could she refuse such a simple request? She wasn't able to support the church with large donations or take part in many of the activities. Making a few cookies was the least she could do.

"I'll be happy to," she agreed, hoping she didn't sound as reluctant as she felt.

How on earth was she going to bake enough to fill all her orders and still donate cookies for the retreat? She felt weary just thinking about it. She loved baking but had never anticipated how much work it was to be successful in her business.

"Bless you," Mrs. Horning said. "I'm sorry you can't join us, but maybe another year."

Before the service began, Shelley sat in one of the cushioned chairs in the sanctuary and silently prayed for the strength to do all that was asked of her. She thanked the Lord for the opportunity to have her own business in a beautiful new kitchen, but she didn't want it to interfere with being a good mother, wife, friend, and Christian.

When the service was over, she intended to hurry home to see how Aiden was, but it was a friendly church. People liked to greet each other and chat a little, and lately it was the only time Shelley had to talk to a few of her friends.

She was just zipping up her jacket and getting ready to leave when Louise Harper walked up to the coatrack. Shelley had worked with her on a church committee long enough to know her husband and children attended a different church. Today Louise looked particularly happy. Her salt-and-pepper hair was newly permed, and she was wearing an attractive purple pantsuit with a white silk turtleneck.

"I don't think you've met my oldest daughter," Louise said. "This is Tami, my pastry chef in training. She's been in New York studying at the City Culinary School."

"Nice to meet you, Tami," Shelley said, offering her hand. "A pastry chef—that sounds interesting."

"You two have a lot in common," Louise said, turning toward her daughter. "Shelley has started her own baking business from her home. She's getting quite a good reputation."

"That's wonderful," Tami said enthusiastically. "I'm a long way from having my own business, but it's one of my goals."

She was a tiny young woman, shorter than Shelley, and curly red hair framed an elfin face lightly sprinkled with freckles.

"When will you graduate?" Shelley asked.

"I hope this summer. Right now we're on a break. I won't go back until April, but I'm excited to finish."

"She's been offered an apprenticeship at a New York restaurant," her mother said proudly.

"How wonderful," Shelley said.

"Did you train at a culinary school?" Tami asked as she pulled on a coat of emerald green wool with brass buttons.

"No, I'm self-taught. I don't do anything very fancy. Cookies are my specialty."

"Shelley has a brand-new kitchen on the back of her house," Louise said. "Everyone in the church expects her to do very well."

The praise made Shelley squirm a bit. She chafed at self-promotion, but she knew she had to be more aggressive to build her business.

"I'd love to know how a home baking business works," Tami said. "It must be pretty involved."

"You're welcome to drop by any time and see my kitchen," Shelley politely offered.

"I'd love to! Would it be possible to see it now? Do I have time before Aunt Jean and Uncle Bob come for Sunday dinner, Mom?"

"Maybe this isn't a convenient time for Shelley," Louise said, giving her an out.

"No, it's fine. I'd love to show you where I work. Not many people get excited about ovens and freezers and such. Be warned, though. I have a four-year-old and a toddler with runny noses."

"Not to worry. I never get sick."

"If you're sure, Shelley, I'll drop Tami off at your house and come back for her in about half an hour. I want to make a quick call on an invalid lady who's on our prayer list. It won't be long because she's pretty weak and visiting tires her."

"That would be great," Shelley said, genuinely looking forward to spending time with someone who shared her enthusiasm for baking.

She left ahead of Tami, who was still waiting for her mother to finish talking to a friend. She hoped she had time to pick up abandoned toys on the floor and get the dirty dishes from breakfast into the dishwasher if Dan had forgotten to do it.

"I'm home," she called out as soon as she got in the door.

Prize dashed up and wagged her welcome, but there was no sign of her husband or the kids. She immediately worried that Aiden was seriously ill. Where would Dan go on a Sunday morning with both kids if not to seek medical help?

With her heart in her throat, she looked around for a message. Fortunately Dan had left a scrawled note on the table beside a half-eaten piece of toast and Emma's sippy cup.

"Mom invited us for Sunday dinner at two o'clock. Took the kids early. Aiden feeling fine. No need to bring anything. Love ya, Dan."

His parents meant well, but she was in a time crunch. She absolutely had to mix up several batches of dough to put in the refrigerator to bake the next day. If they spent the whole afternoon with Frances and Ralph, she would have to work in the evening to catch up.

Dan was the youngest in a large, close-knit Maine family. His six siblings had all gone to college and entered professions, so he sometimes felt like the odd man out at family gatherings. She rather hoped none of his nieces or nephews were there. They were all a fair bit older than Aiden and things could be wild when the kids couldn't go outside.

She quickly cleared the table and put the plate and cup in the dishwasher. By the time she'd looked around to be sure everything was in order, the doorbell rang.

"This is so nice of you to show me your kitchen on such short notice," Tami said.

"It's my pleasure. Can I take your coat?"

"Yes, please." The tiny young woman slipped out of the oversized coat and looked around.

"My husband took our two kids to his parents' house," Shelley explained. "The kitchen is back here."

"Mom said you added a whole new room onto the back of the house."

"My father-in-law and husband did the work. This is where the old kitchen was," she pointed out as they walked past the dining table. "When I investigated starting my own business, it was obvious the old kitchen would never be approved by the health department. I worked out of a restaurant here in town for a while, but that wasn't very satisfactory."

"How nice," Tami said, stepping into the room and looking around with a practiced eye. "Is that real marble on the island? It must be convenient for rolling out dough. I like the stainless steel appliances. Oh, you have a commercial grade refrigerator, and look at your mixer. You're certainly up-to-date for a home kitchen."

"My husband gave me the mixer as a gift. At the time it was more welcome than jewelry or clothes—and still is." She chuckled.

"This must be a cheerful room when the sun is shining. We have high intensity lights at my culinary school. It helps a lot in measuring and testing for doneness. Our instructors are really big on precise measurements and exactly the right amount of time in the oven. Do you mind if I look in your fridge?"

"No, help yourself," Shelley said, a little surprised by the younger woman's running commentary.

"I'm a fanatic when it comes to any kind of baking," Tami said with her face practically inside the fridge. "I'm fretting a bit over this monthlong break, but, of course, Mom is happy to have me home. When I'm apprenticing as a pastry chef in New York, it will be hard to get free time."

"It sounds exciting," Shelley said a bit wistfully. She loved her life, her family, her church, and her business, but sometimes she fantasized about living in a big city.

"The school is great with all the most up-to-date equipment. The only drawback is sharing a tiny apartment with three other girls. We hardly have room to turn around, but at least we're all students at the same school. We always have something to talk about. I'd hate to room with people who weren't into culinary arts. The father of one of my roommates owns three high-class restaurants in the city."

"That's nice," Shelley said, wondering what qualified as "high class" in Tami's opinion.

"Do you mind if I open your cupboards? Ms. Cochran, my favorite teacher, says good cooking begins with good organizing."

"Go right ahead," Shelley said.

Tami went from cupboard to cupboard, literally humming to herself as she checked out orderly shelves of dishes and supplies.

"Your spices aren't in alphabetical order. My mother refuses to organize hers that way, but Ms. Cochran insists on it. That way, a chef never has to hunt for the right container."

"I prefer to keep the ones I use most at the front," Shelley said, a bit bowled over by Tami's critique of her kitchen. At least it was interesting to be with someone who understood what was involved in baking.

Her guest paced the room, commenting on everything she saw.

"This is a very workable home kitchen," she said. "You were right to paint the walls a creamy white. It helps make it so light and airy."

"The windows allow me to work and watch my kids play in the backyard. My biggest problem is finding enough time to fill all my orders. I'm truly grateful the business is going well, but some days I wish there were two of me."

"You don't have anyone to help with the baking?" Tami had a thoughtful expression.

"No, it's just me."

"I have an idea." She shook her head. "No, maybe you don't want to hear it."

"Tell me," Shelley said, intrigued by her visitor's flair for the dramatic.

"I'll be in Marble Cove a whole month, and there's not much to do here. My parents are gone working all day, so it's just me in an empty house. I plan to make treats for them, of course, but they both watch their diets. Why don't I come work for you until school starts?"

"It's sweet of you to offer," Shelley said, feeling a bit uncomfortable with Tami's proposal, "but I can't possibly hire you. I'm still in the building stage, and so far the profits won't stretch to pay for extra help, much as I'd like to work with you."

"I didn't mean you should pay me," Tami said with a light laugh. "I'm volunteering to help out just for the chance to bake in your kitchen. I'm so excited about becoming a pastry chef, I can't stand being away from it for a month. Please say yes!"

"I'd love to," Shelley said, "but I wouldn't feel right not paying you."

"Hey, I could be your apprentice. Since I haven't completed all my courses, I certainly can't charge you for letting me play in your kitchen."

"You really want to help me?"

Tami smiled. "I don't dust, vacuum, or do laundry, but I'll do anything in the kitchen: clean the oven, wash out the fridge, whatever you want done."

"I am struggling to keep up with my business and family," Shelley said thoughtfully. "Maybe you're the answer to my prayers."

"Wow, I'm blown away! Just think, we wouldn't have met if you'd left the church a minute earlier—or if I'd decided to go to church with my dad instead of my mom. My sister and I were given a choice when we were old enough, but we both liked the more formal services at Dad's church. I was an acolyte, believe it or not. But for some reason, my mind told me to go with Mom this morning."

"I still feel I'm taking advantage of you."

"Don't! I can't imagine sitting home alone all day watching soap operas or inane talk shows. You'll be saving me from a really boring vacation."

"It's a deal then," Shelley said, still feeling a bit hesitant.

To her surprise, Tami gave her a big hug and danced around the room. She was such a small person, she reminded Shelley of a children's story about elves who came at night and did all the work.

"You've made my break! What time do you want me to start tomorrow?"

"You're a volunteer. You can come any time you like."

"No, that wouldn't be professional. You have to be able to depend on me and schedule what I'm to do."

"Lately I've tried to be in the kitchen by seven. That gives me an hour or so before my children wake up. But there's no reason for you to come so early. How about nine o'clock? They should be fed and dressed by then," Shelley said.

"Do they go to preschool?"

"No, that's not in our budget right now. My husband is laid off, so things are a bit tight."

"You bake with children in the house? I'm impressed!" While she talked, Tami took another look at the collection of spices and went on to stare at a shelf of canned goods. "You have almond paste. That's one of my absolute favorites. Mrs. Bauer—"

"Call me Shelley," Shelley said with a wink. "I'm not that much older than you."

"Shelley, we're going to have wonderful fun together. Oh, I think my mother is honking for me to come out. If one of my boyfriends had done that when I was in high school, she would've had a fit. Of course, she only wanted to check out my dates. Some girls worry about their father not liking a guy, but in our family my mother was the worrier. But that's more than you want to know. I'm so excited I can't stop blabbing."

After Tami hurried out to her mother's car through a soggy mix of rain and snow, Shelley took a minute to catch her breath. She desperately needed another pair of hands to help her keep up with orders, but was it right to let Tami work without pay? She'd never baked with another person, and she wasn't quite sure how to share the workload. It wasn't as if Tami would be her employee.

Could she possibly pay her anything? She wanted to give Adelaide a modest amount so she knew her help was appreciated, but a trained pastry chef would be insulted by the pittance Shelley could scrape up. She would have to take Tami at her word and accept her as a volunteer.

Usually she took some baked treats to her mother-in-law's dinners, but today she simply didn't have anything to spare in the freezer. She got ready to leave, still a little overwhelmed by Tami's offer. She was unsure about what to do with the eager student chef.

Would Tami really be the answer to her prayers? Or would she make Shelley's life even more complicated?

CHAPTER FOUR

When Diane moved to Marble Cove after a cancer scare and her husband's death, she had anticipated a quiet, uneventful life. Instead the small town had proved to be a place full of mysteries and wonderful people. Already she'd formed several close friendships. She'd even found the perfect companion, Rocky, a golden retriever/Lab mix she rescued when he was abandoned. They took to each other immediately, and it was nice to have him as a sounding board. His sweet, patient nature made it seem he understood every word she said.

The icing on the cake was the sale of her first book, a cozy mystery set in a town very much like Marble Cove. The editor had liked it enough to contract her to do two more linked novels.

Unfortunately, she was beginning to see the computer as her enemy. She had a daily routine of checking e-mails and the news on her favorite site. On a good day she spent less than half an hour on this, and then settled down to work on the book.

It'd been too long since she'd had a good writing day. What she wrote one day seemed bland and uninteresting the next. She'd been doing more deleting than creating. Was this writer's block, or was the trouble with the mystery in the book? It didn't seem to be working, although the outline was full of promising situations. She'd had no idea that writing a second book would be more difficult than the first.

"Maybe I'm just not concentrating," she said to Rocky.

Certainly the real world had intruded on her time and thoughts lately. She'd spent a lot of time working on figuring out how to get Orlean Point Light on the National Register of Historic Places. More recently, she was very interested in working with her friend Beverly to help raise money for the renovation of Old First, the oldest church in town. The more she worked on projects like these, the more she believed preserving the past enriched the present.

"I wonder what Beverly is doing today," she said, rewarded by a tail wag from Rocky.

She and Beverly had discovered a boarded-up steeple above a ceiling in Old First when they went there to scope out the buildings for a dinner/silent auction fund-raiser. It had apparently been hidden for many generations and contained a chest with letters written by Jeremiah Thorpe, the man responsible for building Orlean Point Light.

Old First's current minister, Silas Locke, was upset by their intrusion and had shooed them away. Diane was so flustered by his reaction that she had forgotten that she'd hidden the letters on her person and accidentally taken them home. There was no question she would return them to the church eventually, but first she wanted to understand the messages scrawled in faded ink. They hinted at a hidden treasure, and her active imagination saw it as a way to fund the urgently needed renovation of Old First—if they could find it.

With a real mystery on her mind, she couldn't seem to focus on her fictional one. She sat at the computer and sent Beverly a message:

"At loose ends today. Still haven't been able to read all the letters. Jeremiah Thorpe must have flunked penmanship! Do you have time to come over and take another look at them?"

She didn't wait long for an answer.

"I'd love to, but can't do it today. Give me a rain check."

"Any time," Diane responded.

She was about to open her manuscript and make a stab at writing when the doorbell rang. As usual Rocky got to the door of her cottage first and summoned her with an insistent bark.

"Margaret, nice to see you," she said after opening the door. "I was just wishing for some company. Come in. I'll put the teakettle on."

Rocky lingered beside the visitor, always interested in sniffing her slacks for traces of cat.

"I won't stay long," Margaret said. "I know you want to work on your book."

"Believe me, you're not interrupting anything. I can't seem to string two words together lately. Let's have tea in front of the fireplace. It's so wretched outside I needed a warm glow inside, so I started a fire."

"Sounds lovely. I'm chilled to the bone."

"Make yourself at home," Diane said. "I'll brew the tea."

"Your home is so restful. You were inspired when you decorated around your collection of sea glass. On a day like this when the ocean is dark and angry-looking, it's nice to see your cool, calm colors."

"I appreciate the compliment coming from an artist," Diane called out from the kitchen over the clatter of opening cupboards.

"It's a wonderful palette: oyster white, sandy beige, sea-glass green, pale aqua. I love the whole place. Someday we've got to redecorate, especially our living room. It's such a hodgepodge now."

"It's warm and cozy. Oh no! I can't believe I did this!" Diane cried.

"Is something wrong?" Margaret quickly moved to the kitchen.

"No harm done, but I left the stove burner on again. I don't know where my head is."

"You probably had other things on your mind. It happens to all of us," Margaret reassured her.

"It's been happening to me too often," Diane said.

"I get mad at myself for forgetting things too. The most annoying thing I do is go into a room and forget why I'm there. Allan teases me, but sooner or later I remember what I came for. The computer between my ears works a little slower these days."

"Mine has crashed when it comes to working on my book. I don't think I've written one good sentence in the last week."

"This is the beginning of a new week," Margaret reminded her. "After all your years as a reporter, you'll come through just fine. Maybe you need to step back and take a second look at your idea. That's what I do when a painting isn't going well."

"I can't believe you ever paint badly." Diane opened two foil packets and dangled the tea bags in her ivory mugs.

"I make some false starts," Margaret admitted. "Fortunately, I can always block them out with gesso and begin again if I'm working on a canvas board. Paper I just recycle."

Diane poured hot water over the bags and let them brew, then carried two steaming mugs of Earl Grey to the living room.

"Have you heard anything from Beverly lately?" Margaret asked, holding the hot mug a bit gingerly until Diane put a pair of coasters on the occasional table.

"I e-mailed her this morning. I was hoping she could come over and take another look at Jeremiah Thorpe's letters. I've reached the point where I'm stumped. Unfortunately she's too busy right now to play detective with me."

"I admire her for trying to keep up with her job at the State House and launch her own consulting business. I wonder how long she'll be satisfied with the slow pace in Marble Cove."

"Long enough to help us solve this treasure mystery, I hope," Diane said.

"I had the old trunk and the letters on my mind when I woke up this morning," Margaret said. "The more I look at the copies you made for me, the more intrigued I am."

"I know what you mean," Diane agreed, "but Jeremiah was pretty cryptic when he hinted at treasure. Come into my office. I have a card table set up to study them. Maybe we can brainstorm and come up with some new possibilities."

She led the way to her small, somewhat spartan work area. Although the cottage was small, she'd chosen it because there was work space in a separate room. She didn't want her computer table to dominate the living room or her bedroom.

"I keep them in the box you arranged for them, still wrapped in acid-free tissue paper," Diane said. "I don't want them to disintegrate while I have them in my possession."

She took a flat box from a bookcase shelf and set it on her desk.

"I know the drill," Margaret said, taking the seat in front of them while Diane pulled her computer chair up to the table.

"Oh my," Diane said. "Do you know what caused all those reddish-brown spots?"

"It's foxing," Margaret noted. "Book collectors don't like it, but it is a sign of age. Some experts think it's a fungal growth. Others attribute it to the oxidation of iron or copper in the paper pulp."

Diane started to spread out the letters so Margaret could see them better. "Is there a way to get rid of it?"

"I imagine professional restorers could do something. The only home remedy I've heard of is hydrogen peroxide used very lightly with a cotton swab. I don't think we dare try that. A strong chemical might make the ink fade even more. At least, that's my guess."

"It feels strange to be looking at words written by the founder of the lighthouse. I wonder what kind of man he was," Diane said.

"That's the intriguing thing about history. The lives of those who've passed on are endlessly fascinating. I like to imagine living in another age, although women have it much better today," Margaret said.

"If I'd lived when Jeremiah Thorpe did, I certainly wouldn't have been a journalist," Diane mused.

"Life must have been terribly hard. Look at this page. It's an account of three people who died of the 'sickness.' Jeremiah says he fears it was a judgment from God for their sins."

"We're so blessed knowing there's a loving God," Diane said. "When I read about the lives of early Puritans, it gives me chills. Their life was hard in so many ways."

"I know how you feel," Margaret said. "Here, take a look at this page."

Diane read through the spidery lines of writing, frowning at the difficulty of making out the faded brown words. "Was the ink brown when this was written?" she asked.

"No, most likely it was black. Time has taken its toll. I have to admit, I can only make out about half the words, and I'm not too sure about some of those. Still, every time I go over them, I glean a little bit more about Thorpe's intention. They remind me of a light with a dimmer. I'm gradually seeing a bit more over time, sometimes when I least expect it."

"I know what you mean. Sometimes I get clarification of a word or sentence when I least expect it too. A poet I read once wrote, 'Relax and refresh your soul.' To me it means enlightenment comes when you clear your mental screen."

"I never thought of it that way, but it sounds right," Margaret said, still scanning the aged pages. "Maybe that's why I paint my best on the beach. When the sun illuminates the sea and gives a golden hue to the lighthouse, it lulls me into a totally relaxed mood, and my fingers seem to have a life of their own."

"All your paintings are good, but I like the ones you paint on the beach the best," Diane said.

"Thank you. They're my favorites too." Margaret brushed a stand of gray hair away from her forehead and stared at the brownish paper. "Some of the letters must have been written in a big hurry."

"There's also a chance he was writing in secret. The original buildings probably didn't allow for much privacy."

"Good point," Margaret said. "I also noticed his handwriting wavered on some of them. Maybe he was ill when he wrote them."

"Or he was writing by light of a candle and couldn't see well."

"I imagine candles were in short supply. Maybe he was using a little oil lamp. Do you think they would smoke and discolor the paper?" Margaret asked.

"Possibly," Diane said, "but the early settlers wouldn't have had the time or resources to bleach paper, if they made it at all. It probably wasn't white to begin with."

"That's a good point," Margaret said enthusiastically.

Loud barking in the other room suddenly interrupted their conversation.

"Goodness, Rocky," Diane said, hurrying toward the front room. "What's gotten into you?"

She opened the door a crack, but no one was there.

"Hush," she said to the still barking dog. "There's nothing out there."

"Maybe he's telling me it's time to go home," Margaret said with a chuckle.

"It's not like him to bark at nothing," Diane said apologetically. "Please don't feel you need to hurry away."

"Actually, I do need to leave if I'm going to accomplish anything today. The older I get, the faster time goes by. Before I know it, the summer people will be back. I need to finish a good selection of paintings for my gallery before then." She put on her coat and boots while Rocky paced restlessly in front of the door.

As soon as Diane said good-bye to her friend, she went to the back door and let Rocky out. He began investigating the ground where large snow piles had turned to grayish ice under the onslaught of cold rain. Confident that he wouldn't stray far, Diane shut the door and took care of the tea mugs.

A few minutes later she opened the back door and called out.

"Rocky, here, boy! Time to come in before you're soaked."

Somewhat to her surprise, he didn't immediately come bounding toward her. In fact, she had to step outside and look around to see where he'd gone.

"Here, Rocky!" She wasn't worried, but it was too cold and wet to stand outside calling for him.

Diane went back inside and watched for him through the glass window in the door, getting impatient when she didn't see any sign of him.

After a few minutes, she went to the front door and called again, beginning to wonder what he was up to. Had he sensed another dog and given chase? It was lousy weather to be outside. When he did come in, she'd have to dry him down or possibly give him a bath if he'd gotten into anything.

"Rocky!" she called emphatically.

Just when she thought she'd have to go looking for him, he showed up at the door, his fur matted and his paws dirty.

"Bad dog," she scolded, resigned to giving him a bath so he wouldn't leave a trail through the whole house.

She didn't mind the bath, although he wasn't the most cooperative pet, but she did wonder what had made him stray out of sight of the house. Until now, he'd been exceptionally good about not wandering away.

"Are you out solving some mystery of your own?" she asked her canine friend.

CHAPTER FIVE

Beverly stared out her bedroom window, wondering if the sun had forsaken Marble Cove. She wasn't usually fanciful, but she could imagine a great bank of gray clouds settling over Marble Cove like the lid on a pot while the rest of the world basked in glorious sun.

Of course, the Weather Channel told a different story. The whole Northeast was blanketed by dismal weather, and today Maine could expect sleet and driving winds.

One of the things she liked best about being at her father's was running along the beach. Obviously she could forget about it today.

Before going down for breakfast, she quickly checked her image in the dresser mirror. The dampness curled the ends of her dark, shoulder-length hair, which wasn't at all the sleek look she preferred. She was so accustomed to her slender torso she hardly bothered to check it out, but her navy slacks did seem loose this morning. Her waist wasn't noticeable under a heavy white cable-knit sweater, but she didn't like feeling sloppy.

She'd been sorry to turn down Diane's invitation yesterday, but her father's dental appointment had been her top priority. There were still patches of ice on the rain-covered walks, and she hadn't wanted him to go alone. Sometimes he thought she was overly protective, but at seventy-nine, he was getting frail. He struggled with diabetes and had recently been put on medication to minimize the occurrence of ministrokes. Fortunately he was doing very well, because she did put in full days telecommuting for her job at the Augusta State House and working on her new consulting business.

"Time for breakfast!"

Mrs. Peabody's eighty-plus years hadn't affected the volume of her voice, and Beverly hurried to the kitchen where her father's cook and sometime-helper had laid out the morning meal on a yellow plaid tablecloth.

Although Mrs. Peabody was older than Beverly's father, she was energetic and clear-minded. She enjoyed her part-time role in the Wheeland home, and, as Beverly had learned some time ago, she needed the small salary she earned there.

"Looks good," Beverly said as she came into the kitchen.

Her father was already eating his scrambled eggs and cinnamon toast while Mrs. Peabody hovered nearby to be sure he liked it. Beverly wasn't fond of large breakfasts, but she dutifully joined him every morning, complimenting Mrs. Peabody for neatly loosening the segments of grapefruit on her plate.

"I need to go to the library today," her father said between bites. "I'm reading a biography of Paul Revere, and I want to check a few facts."

A retired high school social studies teacher, her father was still an avid reader and meticulous in running down anything he didn't agree with.

"It's miserable out there," Beverly said. "Could it wait?"

"Should clear up by afternoon," he said. "Anyway, when did a Mainer let a little bad weather hold him back?"

Coming from her father, it was a rhetorical question. Beverly knew he'd want to walk, but she'd end up driving him because it really was nasty outside.

"The Mister and I were talking about cleaning the fridge today," Mrs. Peabody said.

"You were talking about it," her father said. He winked at Beverly from behind his paper. He was fond of the older woman, but sometimes her talkative ways annoyed him.

"Well, be that as it may, I can't remember the last time it had a good scrubbing. Happens I can stay longer today to get it done."

"That would be fine," Beverly said.

"I noticed them apples aren't looking too good. Maybe I could use them to cook up some sauce."

"Whatever you like."

Beverly occasionally fixed one of her mother's old recipes for her father, but most of the time she was content to let Mrs. Peabody run the kitchen. Even before her husband's death, she'd preferred the work world to domestic life.

"What are you doing today?" her father asked, folding the paper and laying it beside his plate.

She wasn't sure how to answer. Her life was like a jigsaw puzzle these days, and the pieces weren't fitting together very well. She was feeling stalled at the State House and felt she had done all she could there. Her plans for a consulting business were coming together nicely, but she worried that she might miss the camaraderie of her colleagues when she eventually started consulting full-time.

While she nibbled on a piece of toast, her mind drifted to Jeff Mackenzie, the man she'd been seeing socially. His job as a photographer kept him away quite a bit, but she found herself thinking about him during his absences.

"Penny for your thoughts," Mrs. Peabody said.

Beverly realized she'd been holding the toast for several minutes without taking a bite.

"Not worth the investment," she said with a forced laugh.

The last thing she wanted to do was mention Jeff to Mrs. Peabody or her father. She didn't want either of them jumping to conclusions about their fledgling relationship. She was absolutely certain she didn't want Mrs. Peabody talking about her and Jeff all over town.

"When do you want to go to the library?" she asked her father.

"They don't open until ten." He got up from the table and flicked some crumbs off his green plaid shirt.

"I'd like to run over to Diane's if she has time, but I won't stay long. I'll go with you when I get home. There are some things I'd like to look up myself."

"Suits me," he said, retreating to his study and his books.

Beverly e-mailed her friend and received a warm invitation to come over. The weather was even more wretched than she thought, but she opted to walk the short distance.

Diane was wearing a blue quilted robe and fuzzy slippers when she opened the door.

"Have I come too early?"

Diane chuckled. "No, no, I'm glad you're here. The house was chilly, so I decided to put off my shower until it warms up. Come sit by the fire, and I'll make some tea."

"None for me, thanks, but your fireplace is really inviting. I'm shivering just from walking here," Beverly said, joining her friend in the circle of warmth.

"Margaret came over yesterday," Diane said after they'd exchanged a bit of news. "We were talking about possible reasons why Jeremiah Thorpe's writing was so shaky. He might have been ill or had some sort of condition that made his hands shake, but he could've just been writing in a secret place with very little light."

"I'm going to the library with my father later this morning. I'll see what I can turn up about the early settlement. Maybe it would help us if we had a better picture of what life was like at the time."

They chatted for several minutes about inconsequential things, and Beverly found it soothing to be with a good listener like Diane. She wanted the visit to go on, but the cell phone in her purse interrupted the tranquil visit.

"Sorry, I'd better take this. My father may be getting impatient to go to the library," she said, rummaging in her big leather bag.

"Hello?" She listened intently and with disbelief as the person on the other end spoke for several moments.

"Yes, of course. I understand what a great opportunity it is."

Diane had discreetly left the room, but Beverly was too mesmerized by the voice on the other end to say much herself.

"I need time to think about it," she said at last, not quite believing what she'd heard.

"Thank you. I really appreciate it," she said at the conclusion of the conversation.

She caught herself clutching her phone so hard her knuckles were white. "Yes, I'll check my e-mail for the details as soon as I get home. Thank you so much."

She was still holding her phone when Diane came back into the room.

"Is something wrong?"

Beverly shook her head, still trying to process all she'd heard.

"Is your father all right?"

"Oh yes, it wasn't about him." She dropped the phone back into her purse. "I'm afraid I have to cut our visit short. Something has come up."

She very much wanted to confide in her friend, but it was too soon.

"Something good, I hope." Diane walked to the front door with her, escorted by Rocky, who was being uncharacteristically quiet.

"Maybe." She frowned as she pulled on her coat. "Sorry. I'm not trying to be mysterious. It was a job possibility, but it came so much out of the blue I don't quite believe it. I need to go home and check my e-mail for the details. I'll probably talk your ear off about it when I know more."

"Any time you want to talk, I'm here," Diane said.

"I really appreciate your understanding."

Beverly stepped out into the foul, windblown sleet, but she scarcely noticed the icy stings on her face. She walked fast, wanting to run but held back by the possibility of slipping and falling.

When she came into the kitchen through the back door, Mrs. Peabody had the entire contents of the fridge spread out on the counters. She was busily washing out the produce drawer, the sleeves of her brown raglan sweater pushed up over bony elbows.

"You're just the one I need. I think this squash has gone bad, but the Mister says no. He doesn't know diddly about produce."

"Neither do I," Beverly quickly said. "You make the decision."

"Well, if that's the way you feel."

Beverly was too anxious to talk about vegetables. She'd probably have to apologize later because she knew she sounded rude, but now she had to get to her computer.

All the way home she'd wondered whether she'd heard right. Maybe she'd read more into the conversation than had been intended. Maybe she was swayed by wishful thinking.

There was something about seeing words on the computer screen that made the surprising offer seem more genuine. She sat down and read the message waiting for her.

The sender was J. P. Grother, a well-known headhunter. His firm found high-end jobs with prestigious companies, ones that couldn't be approached by ordinary means. She'd sent her resume to him many months ago and had heard nothing except a sentence saying it had been received. She'd never expected to hear from him and had, in fact, forgotten about contacting him.

"Come on, come on," she said when her e-mail was slow coming online. All she needed was to lose her Internet, which was not an impossibility when Marble Cove was under siege by the weather.

After what seemed like ages but was more likely seconds, she was able to open J. P. Grother's message.

He was recommending her for a position with a leading pharmaceutical company. Her financial skills were a perfect match for the job, and she was one of only two people on the short list. She would be contacted in the near future for an interview.

She read through a rather lengthy description of the job and saw two downsides: she would have to give up the consulting business she was working hard to build up, and it would require a move to Chicago.

The prospect was exciting, and it was the kind of upscale job she'd dreamed about at one point in her career. Chicago was a vibrant city and a hub for transportation as well as business, but a big disadvantage was the distance from Marble Cove. Could she move that far away from her father? How difficult would it be to fly home for frequent visits? He would be the first to say "take it," but was it a feasible arrangement?

She felt lightheaded with so much to think about. What would she have to give up, and what would she gain? Would a job in Chicago mean a brighter future or a lonelier life? Did she want to give up the independence that the prospect of her own consulting business gave her? And, somewhere in the back of her mind, she wondered, what would a move to the Midwest mean to her budding relationship with Jeff?

"Mom, how I wish I could talk this over with you," she said aloud.

She'd been very close to her mother, and her death a year after Will's had been devastating. Beverly loved her father, but he couldn't take the place of her wise, loving mom. Nor did she have siblings or grandparents to share her doubts and excitement. She even envied Mrs. Peabody her close relationship with her sister.

"I'm looking on the bad side," she told herself, realizing she did have very good friends in Marble Cove, women who could relate to her situation. She had begun to think of them almost as sisters.

She wouldn't just be leaving her father if she went to Chicago. She'd miss Diane's warm companionship, Margaret's wise approach to life, and Shelley's youthful enthusiasm.

"This is all premature," she said aloud, talking to herself in a way she seldom did. "First I have to get an actual offer."

Before then, and it could take a long time, she certainly would discuss the pros and cons with her friends. Would her life be better if she gave up her telecommuting job and her hopes for a consulting business of her own and left Marble Cove? Or was it a decision she would regret?

Chapter Six

Mama!" Aiden cried out from his room as Shelley struggled to put Emma into her snowsuit. "Can I take my cars?"

"You know your grandmother has things for you to play with at her house. You need to put your coat on now."

Emma stiffened in protest, and Shelley struggled to get her daughter's feet into the correct legs of her pink fleece winter wear.

"Just three. Can I take three?"

"Aiden, Daddy will be back any minute to take you to Meemaw's house. It doesn't take long to get gas. Come out here now."

"Two, Mama? Can I take two?"

Shelley shook her head, and Aiden shuffled out of his room and into the foyer, his pants pockets full of the little cars he loved.

"Meemaw just has baby stuff," he protested.

"What about the nice fire truck that used to be Daddy's?"

"It's not fun when I can't play in the sandbox."

"Pappy will be there. If you're good, maybe he'll play a game with you."

"I don't want to play dumb games." He plopped down on the floor and pouted instead of getting into his coat.

"Please, honey, it was nice of Meemaw to invite you to her house. You know you'll have a good time when you get there. I bet she'll make mac and cheese for lunch. Maybe you can help her make brownies too."

Her son stood up with a great show of reluctance and started pulling on his coat. She knew it was only a ploy to get his way. He loved going to Dan's parents' house, and they had plenty of toys to entertain him.

"Honey, you always forget to bring your cars home when you take them. Then you don't have anything to play with here."

"I won't forget."

"Tell you what. You can take two cars with you, but if you leave them there, no one is going to bring them home for you. Now take the rest out of your pockets."

He started spilling the little metal vehicles over the floor, and she decided it would be quicker to pick them up herself than to get him to do it. It might not be good parenting, but she was too rushed to worry about it. Tami Harper was due to arrive soon, and Shelley had only a vague idea about what she wanted her to do.

Having an assistant was a wonderful idea, but she wasn't sure how to use her. Should they work together on the same recipe with Tami measuring and stirring while Shelley put the dough on pans and timed the cookies in the oven? Or would it be more efficient to work on separate orders, perhaps letting Tami mix up the birthday cake that had to be ready tomorrow?

"Are the kids ready?" Dan asked, sticking his head through the entryway without coming inside.

"Almost. Just let me check the diaper bag. I left it in Emma's room. Here, take her."

Dan stepped inside and stood on the mat by the door so he wouldn't track dirt and snow on the floor.

"I told my mom we'd be there by eight thirty."

"Yes, I know," Shelley said, stuffing a spare outfit in the bag as she walked. "I'm doing my best, Dan."

"Shell, don't get bent out of shape. I know getting the kids ready is a big job."

"It was nice of your mother to offer to take the kids today, but she hates people to be late. Here. I think I remembered everything. I told Aiden he could take two cars. Let's hope he'll remember to bring them home. When will you be back?"

"Not sure. I'm going to talk to a guy about a little part-time work. It's worth a shot, but don't get your hopes up."

"Remember I need you to deliver a birthday cake tomorrow."

"Right, the ninety-year-old guy. I didn't forget."

Shelley watched her gang leave and sighed with relief. She didn't like sending them off to her mother-in-law's. Aiden was beginning to resist leaving his own home and toys, and Emma was cross from teething, but she couldn't expect Adelaide to be a full-time babysitter. There was simply no way she could run her business without help with the children. Dan was good about it when he was home, but he had been hitting the pavement in search of work. And when he was home, he often used the Internet to find local jobs, but he got restless when he was inside too much.

She checked the lighthouse clock on the wall in the dining area, one of many lighthouse objects and pictures she'd collected to decorate her house. Tami was due in about fifteen minutes, so she hurried into the kitchen to review the orders to be filled today.

"Don't forget cookies for the women's retreat," she reminded herself, wondering if the best idea was to mix up dough and refrigerate it until Thursday.

Her strategy was to take out the pans, bowls, and other equipment needed for her first recipe. She liked to keep a sink of hot soapy water so she could wash her implements as she went. That way, she was always ready for the next creation. She read through her order slips and decided to begin with chocolate cheesecake. She took out the cream cheese to soften and wondered whether to give Tami the job of crushing the chocolate cookies for the crust.

The doorbell rang before she was halfway ready to give her new helper an assignment.

"Good morning," Tami said, a broad smile on her diminutive face.

Her fiery red hair was drawn back in a tight bun, and she was wearing a white chef's jacket under her open coat.

"Come in," Shelley said, using self-restraint not to chide her for being early. The younger woman wasn't married and had no idea how hard it was to get two children ready for the day.

"I can't tell you how happy I am to be able to bake while I'm on break. It's all I think about these days. I'm nervous and excited and flustered, all at the same time, just thinking about the apprenticeship waiting for me when I finish my classes. I've seen the kitchen where I'll be working, and it's a wonderland for a pastry chef like me, all gleaming white with more counter space than I ever dreamed of having. Imagine, they hire people to clean up after the chefs. Washing up is my least favorite part."

Tami seemingly said all that without pausing to take a breath, and Shelley felt a bit winded just listening to her.

"Let me hang up your coat," she said.

"It's dripping wet. Just spread it out somewhere to dry."

Shelley couldn't see using the heavy wool coat as a rug, so she put it on a hanger and carried it into the bathroom to hang on the shower rod and drip into the tub.

"I shouldn't have walked," Tami told her, "but my car is being serviced, and Mom wasn't ready to drive me. I couldn't wait to get here."

"I've been thinking about how we should do this," Shelley said, leading the way into the kitchen. "I don't know which will work better: teaming up on the same recipe or each doing a separate one."

"I'm totally at your disposal," Tami said, circling the kitchen like a kitten marking its territory. "I'll do whatever you want me to."

"I have an order for chocolate cheesecakes for an upscale restaurant," Shelley said, not quite able to keep satisfaction out of her voice. "I thought maybe you could work on the crusts while I make the filling."

"Just tell me what to do."

"I use a thin chocolate cookie crust. They have to be crushed fine, if you'd like to start doing that."

"Sure, should I work on your marble top island?" Tami asked. "I like a surface that's easy to wipe clean. Wooden cutting boards require quite a bit of upkeep to be sanitary."

Shelley couldn't help but wonder if Tami's over-the-top enthusiasm would last all day. She gave her the repurposed Boy Scout popcorn tin where she stored cookies.

"Oh, they're store-bought," Tami said with a note of disappointment. "If you like, I can whip up a batch of homemade in no time at all. I have a recipe in my head for supercrisp cookies made with squares of unsweetened chocolate."

"Those will work fine," Shelley assured her. "There isn't time to make others for the crust."

"I suppose they'll do," Tami said. "Of course you know what your customer wants. Should I add some spice? Maybe cinnamon and cloves with just a touch of freshly ground nutmeg."

"That's a good idea, but the restaurant was very happy with just a thin crust of plain chocolate cookies. There is the cost of making it to consider."

"Of course! I shouldn't have tried to embellish your recipe. You're the one who knows what's popular in Maine."

Tami hummed while she worked. At first Shelley thought it was nice to see someone who was so happy doing what she did, but after a while she wondered how to tell her helper the tuneless sound annoyed her.

"Sometimes I listen to music on the radio while I bake," she said.

"I have music in my head when I'm working," Tami said with a giggle. "But it won't bother me if you want it."

Shelley turned on the small radio on the counter, but she couldn't find a setting with all music and no commercials. After a few minutes she turned it off without comment. At least Tami had stopped humming.

Her helper had the crusts ready before Shelley finished blending the smooth and tasty chocolate filling. She was beginning to feel a little rushed, so she took a deep breath and told herself she didn't have to race Tami. It took time to make wonderful things, and there was no point in hurrying.

"What now?" Tami asked.

"You can start on a birthday cake. It's for a ninety-year-old man, and his wife wants it to be just like the ones she used to make for him. I laid out a recipe over there," she said, indicating the counter space under her order rack. "I'll be through with the mixer in a minute or so."

"*Hmm*," Tami said thoughtfully. "I think I'll hand beat this one. That way I can gauge the amount of flour as I go. I think this recipe calls for a tad too much."

"Are you one of those bakers who don't measure?" Shelley asked out of curiosity. "I had an aunt who worked that way.

Sometimes she hit a home run, but she had a few failures along the way too. Since I'm running a business, I can't afford to experiment. People expect consistency."

"I'll follow the recipe exactly, although I don't think I've ever ruined a cake—well, maybe once in the eighth grade. I had seen a TV show about using mayonnaise as shortening, but I didn't realize my mom's was low fat. It tasted okay but I'd be embarrassed to do one like it today."

Shelley scraped the last of the filling into one of the crusts and put both cheesecakes into the oven, happy to have one order under control. With Tami doing the cake, Shelley had time to work on the cookies she routinely made for the Cove. She liked to give the restaurant a good variety made from her best recipes. Once a fisherman's pub, it was now a delightful little coffee shop with original worn pine floors and wood-paneled walls. Not only had the owners bought her first commercially made cookies, they'd let her use their kitchen while her new one was being built.

In the rush of getting the kids ready to go, she hadn't had time to decide what kind of cookies to make for her steady customer. Peanut butter usually sold quite well, but she'd made those last week. Of course, anything chocolate virtually, jumped out of the glass display case. She located her oatmeal chocolate chip recipe on her kitchen computer and printed it out, although she did know it by heart. Still, when she was selling a product, she wanted the security of seeing the recipe in front of her as she worked.

Before Shelley could finish mixing the cookies, Tami had the two round cake pans ready to go into the oven.

"The cheesecakes won't be done for at least twenty-five minutes," Shelley said, realizing she hadn't thought of how much oven space it would take with two of them working. Usually her roomy new oven was more than adequate to keep up.

"What should I do next?" Tami asked, sounding eager to begin something else.

"We're backed up a little on the baking. If you wouldn't mind, I have some walnuts in the shells. The supermarket had a special, and I haven't had time to crack them. They're in the cupboard by the mixer. I need small pieces, so you can use the nut chopper in the big drawer to the left of the sink. Oh, I also like to keep up with dishwashing as I go. It should work well if we both do our own."

Even though Tami had agreed to do any job in the kitchen, Shelley didn't think she'd take kindly to being the dishwasher.

Tami started humming again as she tackled the walnuts with a small hand nutcracker Shelley had found at a garage sale.

"What are you going to do with them?" she asked as she fed the halves into a small nut grinder. "My, this is going to take a long time."

Shelley hoped it would. Tami was a little whirlwind when she worked, but the kitchen was set up for one baker. It was good to have help, especially when orders were stacked up, but there wasn't much the fledgling pastry chef could do until the oven and mixer were free.

By the time the cheesecakes came out and the birthday cake went into the oven, Tami had finished the walnuts, washed the bowls and pans, and scrubbed everything in sight.

"The customer wants an egg white icing, something light and fluffy and not too sweet," Shelley said as she dropped spoonfuls of cookie dough onto a pan. "I printed out a recipe called Angel Icing. Maybe you can have a look at it before the cake is cool enough to frost."

It was lunchtime when the cakes did come out, but Shelley didn't have time to stop.

"Why don't you make yourself some lunch now? There's sliced turkey and cheese in the fridge, and the mixed grain bread is pretty good. You can grill it in my toaster oven if you like."

"Oh, I never bother eating when I'm working. It dulls my palate, and I think it's terribly important to taste things like frosting. Once I left the vanilla out of a cream puff filling. You can be sure I sample everything now."

Shelley made it a point not to nibble while she baked. She worked hard to stay slender, and a bite here and there could add up, although Tami's sampling didn't seem to have affected her at all. She was as slim as she was short.

For the rest of the afternoon, orders flew off Shelley's oven rack. Thanks to Tami, she wouldn't have to work that evening except for a little bookkeeping, never her favorite job.

"I've had a wonderful time," the young pastry chef said as she left for the day. "Is it all right if I come at the same time tomorrow? I'm always up by seven, and there's nothing to do once my mom goes to work."

"Happy to have you," Shelley said as she brought Tami's coat to the foyer. "I don't always have quite that much to do though."

"I have a mystery recipe I've been dying to try. If there's time this week, would you mind it I made it in your kitchen? Working in my mother's is like being in a time warp. I'm afraid I've gotten spoiled by the state-of-the-art facilities at my culinary school. Actually, I was surprised to see some of the modern features in yours. Of course, I'll bring the ingredients myself."

"No problem," Shelley said, wondering what Tami considered a mystery recipe.

When the door closed on her new helper, Shelley felt like collapsing where she stood. Managing a volunteer wore her out. What would she do if she ever actually hired someone to work for her?

CHAPTER SEVEN

"I wonder whether Shelley will let me help her make something today," Adelaide said at the breakfast table Wednesday.

"Maybe not today," Margaret said as she cleared away her daughter's cereal bowl. "Shelley has a young lady helping her while she's on vacation from cooking school. Her mother, Mrs. Harper, told me when I went to the market."

"Sometimes she lets me mix cookies while Aiden and Emma are sleeping," Adelaide said.

Margaret smiled lovingly at her daughter. "You have a much more important job watching the kids."

"But, Mom. Shelley showed me how to drop cookie dough on the pan," Adelaide said, sounding a bit distressed at the prospect of not helping in the kitchen.

"I know, dear. I'm sure once Shelley's new helper is back at school you'll have a chance to do some more baking. In the meantime you're going to the community center this morning. Daddy will drive you after he gets back from the hardware store."

"I like going to the hardware store."

"Yes, I know, but Daddy wanted to go early. You were still in your pajamas."

As Margaret absentmindedly chatted with her daughter, her thoughts were on all the things she'd left undone in recent days, not the least of which was talking to Beverly about exercise programs. She knew she was procrastinating. As much as she needed a meaningful workout in her life, the prospect brought back memories of physical education classes in school. She always did well in swimming, but she was hopelessly awkward in gymnastics and sports.

She had visions of a roomful of women exercising in sync while she was out of step and struggling to keep up. There had to be a way to get in better shape without exposing her awkwardness.

When Adelaide went to her room to get ready for Allan's return, Margaret went to the kitchen window and stared out at the uninviting weather. It had stopped raining, but a cold wind was shaking the bare branches of the neighbor's tree. Last year's garden was a tangle of colorless stalks, and the remnants of snow piles were dingy gray. Her fingers itched to get outside and start planting, but it would be many weeks before it was warm enough for Allan to plow up the ground for her.

Meanwhile, she didn't want to brave the wind and cold to walk outside, and it would be months before it was warm enough to swim in the ocean. Still, this was her best time of year for exercise. The gallery was only open part time, since most sales were to summer people. Although she was working steadily on her paintings, she still had time to begin a serious exercise program if she could just muster up enough enthusiasm.

"Is Adelaide ready to go?" Allan asked as he walked into the kitchen with his winter jacket buttoned up to his throat. "She'll need her quilted winter coat."

"Yes, of course. I washed her red mittens yesterday, but they should be dry. I'll get them, but first I wanted to talk to you about something. It slipped my mind yesterday, but Shelley offered again to pay Adelaide for watching her children."

"But we agreed she's doing us a favor by having her. Adelaide loves being with the kids," he said.

"Yes, but Adelaide has never really had money of her own to manage. We always handle her gift money and take her shopping to spend it. Maybe it would be a good experience if she actually had a small amount she earned herself."

"We've tried to teach her money skills, but I guess it's not the same as having some of her own. What do you think we should do?"

"I told Shelley we'd only accept a small amount. She suggested giving her a few dollars a day," Margaret said.

He shrugged out of his coat and was quiet for several moments. Allan was very thoughtful, and Margaret counted on him for his wise decisions.

"Maybe it would be a workable idea. Anything we can do to make Adelaide more independent is good. We have to face the fact that we won't be here to care for her forever."

Allan was right, but his reminder made Margaret even more conscious of her own health. She needed to exercise to extend her life as long as possible.

"I'll tell Shelley," Margaret said. "Meanwhile, we'll have to come up with a plan to teach her how to manage small sums."

"I can't find my red mittens," Adelaide said, coming into the room with a look of distress on her face.

"There's still on the drying rack," Margaret said. "They should be dry, so I'll get them for you."

When she came back into the kitchen, her daughter and husband were giggling together. She stood back a few moments and watched, thanking God for their loving relationship. It made her even more determined to take better care of herself. Her recent health scare had upset Allan, and she didn't want a repeat of that any time soon.

"My red mittens!" Adelaide said, putting them on even though she'd have to take them off again to zip up her coat.

Getting ready to go outside in bad weather was a slow process, but Margaret and Allan had both agreed long ago to let her do anything she could manage by herself, no matter how long it took. When they were ready to leave, Margaret hugged her daughter and planted a quick kiss on Allan's cheek. Sometimes the love she felt for both of them was too overwhelming for words.

Adelaide's black-and-white cat Oreo came into the kitchen on delicate paws and investigated the feeding dish. Margaret gave her fresh water and spooned the remainder of a can of cat food into the dish, but her mind was on her schedule for the day.

She was halfway through a winter scene of the lighthouse, and she wanted to finish it this week. Matt Beauregard had recently approached her about using her images on merchandise beyond greeting cards and she wanted to come up with some new pieces for him to purchase. That meant getting a lot of work done before the tourist season began and she was busy at the gallery.

A photo of the unfinished scene was on her table, and she studied it for a few minutes. She needed to work on the sparkle of sunlight on the snow, but she also needed to add a punch of color. A child in a red coat might work, but no one would let a small girl wander alone on the beach. What else could she add?

When inspiration evaded her, she decided to put her work on hold for a little while. She felt listless and anything but inspired.

"Face it," she told herself. "I absolutely have to get more exercise."

She went to the phone and punched in Beverly's number, only intending to ask her about the best exercise option.

"Are you at home?" her friend asked, sounding a bit hurried.

"Yes. I wanted to talk to you about something. Do you have time to stop over for a cup of coffee?"

"Oh, Margaret, I got your message. I've been meaning to call you. I'm so sorry. Yes, of course I can stop over. Are you at home now? Is everything okay?"

Beverly sounded uncharacteristically flustered, so Margaret assured her friend that all was well.

"I don't want you to go to any trouble," Beverly said. "I can be over there in half an hour."

Allan returned before Beverly got there, but he only filled his thermos with coffee before going out to his workroom. He'd been working hard on his line of handcrafted furniture, much of which would go on display in the gallery when the summer season began.

When she'd first met Beverly, Margaret had been a bit daunted by her sleek professional aura. Slender and polished, Beverly always looked put-together. Her dark shoulder-length hair was flattering even when she pulled it back to run, and she managed to look well dressed in her most casual outfits.

Her attitude had felt intimidating at first, but the longer Margaret knew her, the more she discovered the genuine warmth behind Beverly's cool exterior. She was eager to have a nice visit with her.

Beverly arrived looking unusually pink-cheeked.

"That chill goes right through a person," she said, rubbing her hands together as Margaret hung up her green nylon jacket. "I should've worn my ski pants instead of jeans. It always feels colder here than in Augusta."

"I hope our weather won't drive you back to the capital," Margaret said. "We'd miss you!"

Beverly gave her an odd little look, then glanced around the room. "Your front room is so cozy," her visitor said. It felt like a change of subject.

"That's a kind way of saying messy," Margaret said with a chuckle. "The more I pick up, the more things move around. No one would believe this room belongs to an artist."

"I like your jumble of colors. They make me think you have a lively mind and a busy life."

"You're very tactful," Margaret said with smile. "Let's have coffee in the kitchen. I took some pumpkin bars out of the freezer. They should be thawed by now."

"Sounds good. Mrs. Peabody made lumpy oatmeal this morning. I managed to scrape mine into the garbage without her noticing. Fortunately, my father likes almost everything she fixes."

"I really need your advice," Margaret said when they were facing each other across the kitchen table.

"That's scary! I think of you as someone who really has her life on track."

"The truth is, I've put on a little weight this winter. Plus I had a health scare last month. The bottom line is I have to take better care of myself. I've got to find a good way of exercising when it's too cold to swim and too nasty to walk."

"Maine winters aren't conducive to keeping in shape," Beverly said thoughtfully. "I really miss my long runs on the beach."

"But you look as fit as ever. Can you tell me how you do it? And maybe give me some hints?"

"The community center has some good classes. I've been going to aerobics, although not as faithfully as I should," Beverly admitted. "It takes a lot of time to do my regular job plus work on setting up the consulting business."

"Aerobics," Margaret said, wrinkling her nose. "I really get frustrated when I can't stay in sync with the rest of the class. I wonder about something like yoga. Have you ever tried it?"

"Briefly, a few years ago. It seemed a little tedious. I like moving fast, especially running."

"Walking is more my speed, but winter lasts so long in Maine," Margaret sighed.

"I have a friend in Augusta who's in her seventies. She keeps fit by walking on a treadmill," Beverly suggested. "I think Mr. Maker might use one too."

"Allan and I have thought of buying one, but we've been putting all our spare cash into making a success of the gallery."

"Tell you what," Beverly said, sipping coffee from a mug. "I'll check around and see what the options are in Marble Cove. People are pretty health-conscious around here. I'm sure there must be a program somewhere that fits your needs."

"I don't want to take a lot of your time."

"You won't. It's a subject that interests me too. I hate to hurry away, but I'd better go. I don't want to be away from home too much this week."

"Is your father feeling poorly?" Margaret asked, concerned.

"No, nothing like that. I'm just expecting a phone call."

Margaret was curious about a call Beverly didn't want to take on her cell, but she didn't want to pry into her business. Her friend did tend to keep things to herself. She located Beverly's coat in her crowded closet and thanked her for anything she could suggest about an exercise program.

"What are friends for? Someday I may come to you for advice," Beverly said.

After she left, Margaret wondered what advice she could possibly give her new friend. Beverly always seemed so decisive and sure of herself. Margaret often wished she had her self-confidence and energy.

Before she began work on the painting, she had one call to make.

"This is Margaret. I know you're busy so I won't talk long," she said when Shelley picked up her phone.

"Not as busy as you think," Shelley said in a hushed voice. "I have an assistant."

"Yes, Louise Harper told me," Margaret said.

"Hold on. I'll go in the other room."

There was a long pause before Shelley spoke again.

"I'm in my bedroom with the door closed. I didn't want to talk about my helper in front of her."

"Is something wrong?"

"No, I'm just not used to being a boss, not that my assistant needs to be told anything."

"I never expected you to take on help." She didn't want to mention Adelaide's pique at being replaced in the kitchen.

"I haven't! Tami Harper is visiting her mother on break from culinary school. She doesn't want to be away from baking for a month, so she volunteered to help me."

Margaret tried to imagine someone coming into her studio and helping her paint. It would be a nightmare. Was that why Shelley went into her bedroom to talk?

"How is that working out?"

"Oh, she's good. And fast. She doesn't want to be paid, and she has all kinds of ideas for my business." Shelley's tone said more than her words.

"It's still your kitchen," Margaret said, sensing her young friend's distress.

"Oh, I'm just being silly. She's good, really good. Thanks to her, I'm caught up on orders and have time to put some things in the freezer. I'm lucky to have her."

"It's only a temporary arrangement."

"Yes," Shelley said with a sigh of relief. "She's a lovely girl, full of energy—"

"But you like to do things your way. That's why you started your own business."

"You are a wise woman, Margaret," she said, a smile evident in her voice.

"I called about your offer to pay Adelaide. Allan and I talked it over. It really would be good for her to have a small amount of money to manage on her own."

"Great. We're thrilled to pay her. She really is a big help playing with the kids when I'm working in the kitchen."

"We don't want you to give her too much. A couple of dollars a day would be great. That way we can slowly teach her to manage her pay."

"That isn't very much for what she does. Babysitters get a lot more. How about five dollars a day?"

"I guess that would be okay, but please, no more. We want her to be able to go into a store with a little money in her purse and save some as well. We'll see how she manages."

"It's a deal. I feel a lot better giving her something for her work. She helps with folding laundry too. Otherwise, I never seem to catch up. You have no idea how helpful she is."

"Adelaide adores your children."

"She's so gentle and sweet. I couldn't have a better helper!"

Too bad Shelley's baking assistant didn't evoke the same enthusiasm.

CHAPTER EIGHT

O n Saturdays Diane liked to read over everything she'd written during the past five days and flesh out her storyline for the following week. This routine usually gave her a flying start on Monday after a restful Sunday attending church, talking on the phone with her two grown children, Jessica and Justin, and sometimes entertaining friends in the evening.

But the prospects for any out-of-town visitors the second weekend in March were rather bleak. No one wanted to come to Maine when the last of winter was blasting the state, and she wasn't at all happy with what she'd accomplished the previous week.

"I've got to pick up the pace," she said to Rocky as he lay, head between his paws, on the rug in her office.

He responded with a halfhearted wag of his tail, as though he, too, had given up on her second book. Was she going to be a one-book author? Maybe the sale of her first book was a fluke, and she didn't have a second one in her.

As a reporter, she'd never believed there was such a thing as writer's block. It was a luxury she simply could not afford. She'd get an assignment, finish it, and go on to the next.

After all, writing was a skill honed through practice and concentration. Was there a different mind-set for fiction?

She slid her chair from the computer to the card table where Jeremiah Thorpe's letters were tucked away in their acid-free nest so they wouldn't fade in the weak light of late winter. *First do no harm,* she mused. The letters had been hidden in a dark trunk for centuries, and she didn't want them to crumble away before she could think of a way to place them with someone who would restore and cherish them. Unfortunately, it didn't seem like the current minister at Old First had any interest in the history of the church. In fact, he'd been incensed when she and Beverly uncovered the hidden bell tower. She'd only hidden the letters on her person because she'd been trying to get down the ladder, and then she'd forgotten them after his scolding.

She thought of showing them to Pastor Carl at Marble Cove Community Church, the congregation where she was a member, but it didn't seem fair to involve him. She could take them to the public library or the historical society, but it would be too awkward to explain how she happened to have them.

For now, all she could do was try to unravel the vague hints of a long-lost treasure. Something told her it could be the key to raising enough money for the badly needed renovation of Old First, the oldest and most historic church in town and Beverly's special project.

Rocky stood up and restlessly paced the room, stopping to nuzzle her knee, then prowling her office until she got the message: he wanted to go outside.

A dusting of fresh snow had fallen during the night, and the wind was bitterly cold. She thought of taking her canine companion for a walk, but just thinking about it made her shiver. Rocky wasn't all that fond of winter temperatures in spite of his sleek fur coat, so she felt free to let him out on his own.

"No hiding on me this time," she warned, imagining he understood. "Out and in with no wandering away."

She opened the back door, and the Arctic whooshed in as Rocky went out. Was it always this cold in early March? Maybe Marble Cove just seemed more frigid than Boston because there was no urban sprawl to give an appearance of warmth. Or maybe she was more sensitive to low temperatures than she used to be.

Rocky was sniffing the ground, leaving paw prints on the new snow, when she closed the door. She watched him through the window for a minute or two, then took out carrots she needed to clean and chop for the vegetable soup she was going to make in her slow cooker.

She gave him two minutes or so, then went to the door and called him, expecting him to be glad to return to the warm house.

"Rocky! Here, boy! Time to come in."

He bounded toward her and made a beeline for his food dish. She started to close the door when the phone rang. Hoping it was one of her children, she raced toward her cell phone in the office.

A moment later, she returned to the kitchen, disappointed by a call from a telemarketer who wouldn't take no for an answer. To her dismay, she'd forgotten to close the back door. The storm door was slightly ajar, and Rocky was nowhere to be seen. He'd easily pushed through it, thanks to her absentmindedness. Why hadn't she closed both doors and latched them? It would only have taken a second, but she simply hadn't thought of it when she heard the phone.

She surveyed the backyard and saw paw prints going around to the side of the cottage. When Rocky was snowy or wet, she preferred to let him in through the kitchen, but he wasn't giving her a choice. She went to the front door and called again and again, each time more emphatically.

Not only didn't he come, she couldn't see him anywhere on the street. Diane reluctantly stepped outside, shivering in her navy sweatshirt and jeans as she looked in all directions. She could see the Bauer house from where she stood. Rocky had been known to visit their dog Prize, but she didn't see him anywhere in their yard.

Driven inside by the cold, she pulled on her warm lined boots and full-length quilted nylon coat, wrapping a scarf around her head before she put on her warm mittens. She could wait for him to return at his convenience, but she hoped to find him before he got into something that required a bath.

As an afterthought, Diane went to the kitchen intending to get his leash. There was more bad news. She'd recently given him a bath and had neglected to put his collar back on. It was still hanging on the hook with the leash. She was distressed by her carelessness and even more worried about

Rocky. Without his license, he could be treated as a stray. No one would know that he had an owner or how to find her.

Maybe she was going to need a way to tie him up in the backyard, especially if he was going to be an escape artist every time she forgot to close and latch the door. He couldn't get in much trouble in the winter, but once the tourist season started, he'd have to be restrained. She wasn't worried that he might ever hurt anyone, but a big dog bounding through the town might frighten visitors.

Outside the snow had melted on the road, so Rocky's trail ended there. She walked up and down the street, trying to ignore the bite of the wind on her cheeks.

"Rocky!" she called repeatedly, beginning to feel conspicuous.

Her best guess was he'd go toward the ocean. He loved to run on the beach, so she went down to the water's edge, chilled to the bone in spite of her warm clothes. There was no sign of him.

He was fast, very fast, and he could be anywhere by now. Diane half-walked and half-ran back toward town, trying to warm up by moving fast. It didn't work.

Following Newport Avenue to Main Street, she kept her eyes peeled for any sign of her runaway dog. A few people were out shopping, but only the grocery store had many cars parked in the lot. The foul weather was keeping people inside, and that's where she wanted to be.

The chances of spotting him were almost nil. He could be miles away by now, and she was getting colder by the minute. She walked toward home, stopping only to check out the Bauers' backyard, the most likely place for him to hang out if they left the gate open.

No luck. She was more worried than ever, but further searching seemed futile. As she started toward home, Shelley pulled out of the driveway in Dan's truck and stopped to call out to her.

"Diane, were you coming to see me?" she asked.

"No, I'm trying to find Rocky. I accidentally left the back door open, and he took advantage of it. He used to come right in when I let him out, but he's nowhere to be found. I worry he might get hit by a car."

Shelley slid out of the truck and walked over to Diane.

"I'll help you look. Maybe we can spot him from the road."

"That's sweet of you. I guess I can't give up. If he's hurt somewhere..."

"I'm on my way to Margaret's with Adelaide's pay for the week. They agreed to let me give her a small amount for helping with the kids, but I was up to my elbows in dough when she left yesterday. Silly to drive such a short distance, but I have to go grocery shopping afterward. I'm sure Margaret will help look with her van, and I wouldn't be surprised if Beverly wouldn't want to help too."

Diane was encouraged and grateful when Shelley called the other two women and both agreed to bring their cars and join in the hunt.

"We'll meet back at your house in half an hour or so," Shelley said. "Let's hope he hasn't gone farther than we can cover in that amount of time."

Diane slid into the pickup with Shelley, hoping it would be easier to spot Rocky if she didn't have to drive. In spite of checking both sides of the street, she didn't see any sign of him.

"I'll go a little west of town," Shelley said. "Maybe he found a good field for rabbit hunting."

The search proved futile, and Diane had to choke back tears. She loved her pooch, and her days had been much less lonely since her canine companion came into her life. Rocky seemed as happy as she was with the arrangement, so she didn't understand why he'd disappeared.

Margaret and Beverly were waiting in their cars when Shelley stopped in front of her cottage. A quick glance was all she needed to see Rocky wasn't in either car.

"Come inside. I'll whip up some hot chocolate," Diane invited all three friends.

Shelley hesitated briefly, then agreed to come for a few minutes.

"It won't hurt Dan to bond with his children for a little longer," she said.

The four women unbundled with much shivering and stomping of feet.

"It feels colder than it did in January," Margaret complained.

"That damp wind goes right through my coat," Beverly said.

"Come into the kitchen," Diane invited them. "It won't take me long to make some steaming hot chocolate."

"Maybe we could put up posters if Rocky doesn't come home soon," Shelley offered as she watched Diane take out the cocoa powder.

"Good idea," Margaret said. "Allan is pretty good at lettering. I'm sure he'd be happy to make some for you."

"Maybe a little ad in the classifieds would help," Beverly suggested. "Surely someone saw him run through town. If we knew which direction he went, we could track him that way."

"Both ideas are good," Diane said as she stirred chocolate mix into hot milk. "I really appreciate your help. Rocky has never done anything like this before. Usually he comes as soon as I call."

"We'll hope for the best," Shelley assured her.

When the women were settled around the table with mugs of hot chocolate with whipped topping, Diane thought of another reason for all of them to be together. It was a good opportunity to talk about the letters that so intrigued all of them.

"Margaret and I were speculating about why Thorpe's handwriting is so difficult to decipher," Diane said.

"Yes, maybe he was ill or infirm when he was writing," Margaret said.

"Or he could have been hiding so no one knew he was writing them. It was likely he was writing in very poor light," Diane said. "Anyway, I'm still making out a word here and there when I concentrate on them."

"Maybe you're getting used to Jeremiah Thorpe's handwriting," Shelley suggested. "It's all one big smudge to me, but you've made out quite a bit."

"There's a lot to go," Diane said, "but the references to hidden treasure are legible. If he went to the trouble of mentioning it, he must have made some reference about where it is."

"If there is a real treasure, and if we can find it, we can donate it to Old First. It would be a shame to let such a historic building deteriorate any more than it has," Beverly said hopefully.

"You found the blocked-off bell tower," Margaret said thoughtfully. "Could it be there?"

"I doubt it," Beverly said. "Before Reverend Locke chased us away, Diane had a pretty good look. The trunk with the letters was pretty much the only thing there aside from some dusty frames and some old tools. Unless there was another hidden door or compartment up there."

"I wonder if you could get into it again," Shelley mused.

"Not likely," Beverly said. "We clearly weren't welcome, and it's been boarded up again."

The four of them fell into silence, and Diane felt devoid of ideas. She caught herself staring at her mug of hot chocolate as the whipped topping melted into white swirls. Margaret said something, but she had to ask her to repeat it.

"Sorry," Diane said. "My mind has been miles away these days."

"You're probably just worried about Rocky," Shelley said in a kind voice.

"Yes, this is another roadblock for my new book. I don't know how I can possibly concentrate when I'm worried sick about Rocky."

"That's a shame," Shelley said. "Success always seems to have a downside. I have more orders than I dreamed possible, but life seems more complicated now. I have a volunteer helper, in case you didn't know. She's a really good pastry chef, but I'm not sure how to keep her busy and still do the things I want to do."

Margaret made a sympathetic sound, but Beverly seemed far away, lost in her own thoughts.

"How are things coming along with your consulting business?" Diane asked her.

"Oh, it has possibilities." She didn't sound convinced, but Diane didn't want to press her.

"Hot chocolate really hit the spot," Shelley said, "but I have to get to the market if my gang is going to eat this week. Aiden is going through a fussy streak. All he wants for dinner is mashed potatoes and little Vienna sausages. Fortunately, he likes the dehydrated spuds, but I'm all out."

"Thanks so much for looking for Rocky," Diane said as she walked her to the door.

"Don't worry. I'm sure he'll turn up," Shelley reassured her. "I mean, how can a dog that big disappear in our little town?"

"I hope you're right." Diane gave her an affectionate hug and made sure to close the door after her.

"Locking the barn door after the horse has gotten out," she said to herself with a rueful smile.

"Do you have a piece of paper?" Beverly asked when she returned to the kitchen. "Silly question. You wouldn't be a writer if you didn't have a supply."

"Will my kitchen pad do?" Diane ripped off the page with her shopping list and put it on the table with a pencil.

"I thought we could make a list of all the possible places where Jeremiah Thorpe could've hidden something of value," Beverly said.

"What a good idea!" Diane felt a stirring of enthusiasm after her horrible morning. "I would put the beach as number one. Pirates often buried their ill-gotten loot along the shoreline. Why not Jeremiah?"

"It would be awfully hard to remember the place with all that sand," Margaret said in a practical voice.

"My father says there are caves somewhere under Marble Cove. That would be my best guess," Beverly offered.

"If we don't know where they are, I wonder if Jeremiah did," Margaret said.

"If I were going to hide something, I'd still want to keep it close in case I had to get it in a hurry, say in a raid by hostile natives. I'd bury it under my house," Beverly suggested.

"Or maybe in a root cellar, if they had them in those days," Margaret added.

"We have a pretty good list," Beverly said with satisfaction. "I wonder about the church. Thorpe was the spiritual leader. Maybe he would want the treasure to rest in a holy place."

"So many possibilities," Diane said.

"You're the writer. You have the best imagination," Margaret said. "Can you think of someplace really creative?"

"If it's buried outside, there would have to be a landmark so he could find it easily. The trouble is, the terrain must have changed a great deal. How many trees in town are that old?"

"Not many, but it's worth looking into," Beverly said.

"We're thinking about buried gold or jewels, but I don't think the early settlers were rich. Maybe Jeremiah's idea of treasure is something entirely different," Diane said.

"Good point," Beverly said. "What would the first settlers value the most?"

"Food, certainly, and muskets for hunting," Margaret said.

"There was a lot of sickness. Medicine would be high on the list," Diane said. "A store of old remedies might have some historical value, but it seems unlikely Thorpe would've called it a treasure."

"Maybe they traded for something of value. Native Americans had a big trading network. It could be anything from shells to gold nuggets." Beverly made another column on the paper and started adding possible treasures.

"We really don't have a clue," Diane said with a rueful laugh, "but it's certainly fun to speculate."

"We're back at square one," Margaret said pragmatically. "Unless the letters spell out the location, we'll never find the actual treasure."

"I'm not giving up," Beverly said. "How else can we raise the funds to restore Old First? Money is pretty tight these days, and we can't expect people to attend another fund-raiser so soon."

"I should go home," Margaret said. "Allan will be wondering what happened to me."

"Me too," Beverly said. "Now that I'm fortified with your delicious hot chocolate, I can face whatever Mrs. Peabody has concocted for lunch. When I left home, she was peeling enough potatoes to feed a regiment. I'm hoping for potato soup. Father likes it, and it will take us through tomorrow when she doesn't come."

Diane walked her two friends to the door, helping them with their coats.

"I'm sure Rocky will find his way home," Margaret said in a sympathetic voice. "I know how much he means to you."

"Thank you so much, both of you," Diane said as they were leaving. "I really appreciate your help, and you're probably right about Rocky coming home on his own when he's ready."

When her friends were gone, Diane felt at loose ends. She washed the hot chocolate mugs and went to her office, hoping a good idea for the next chapter would strike her like lightning. She pulled up the first chapter and read over it several times, wondering why the hook didn't quite ring true.

After a few minutes, she gave up and turned to the letters on the card table. What did it say about her writing when a puzzle several hundred years old was more engrossing than the mystery in her book?

She looked down at the floor where Rocky usually lounged while she wrote, and a lump filled her throat. Worry about her beloved canine companion gnawed at her, and she couldn't get a handle on any of the ideas floating just beyond her conscious mind. Why couldn't she concentrate? Was she getting too old to fulfill her dream of being an author?

"Dear God, help me to get my mind on straight," she prayed, and then added, "and please let Rocky return home safely."

The last thing she wanted was another loss in her life.

CHAPTER NINE

Had she only been gone two days? Beverly felt as though her whole world had been turned upside down during her short stay in Chicago.

Diane was waiting for her outside the security gate at the Bangor airport.

"I can't tell you how much I appreciate this," she said, hugging her friend. "It's so nice to see a friendly face after all of that traveling. I really don't like my father going outside the town limits in his car anymore, but he would've insisted if you hadn't offered to come get me."

"I'm happy to do it," Diane said. "The trip gave me time to think about something besides Rocky. The house is too quiet to concentrate without him."

"You still haven't found him?"

"No, I don't have a clue where he could be. He's such a beautiful dog. Surely someone would spot him and call animal control. I check with them every day, and Leo promised to enlist his dog-loving clients in the search," Diane said.

"Of course, Dr. Spangler. How is he these days?" Beverly asked. "Has he asked you out again?"

"Now, Beverly, you know we're just friends," Diane answered and then quickly changed the subject. "But tell me about your trip."

"My plane was late, so I had to change for my appointment in an airport restroom instead of going to my hotel for a leisurely shower first."

"Oh no," Diane said sympathetically. "That's an awful way to get ready for an interview."

"It gets worse. I ended up with a cabby who got lost, of all things. Or maybe he took a wrong exit to get more miles on the meter. The interview was at a plant near Schaumburg, which is way north of the city. If I'd had time to figure it out, I would have done better taking a commuter train, but by that time I really had to hustle."

Beverly pulled her wheeled overnight bag as she talked, following Diane's lead to her car in the parking lot.

"Tell me about the interview," Diane prompted.

"Things got much better when I connected with the vice president in charge of human resources and her assistant. They took me to an upscale French restaurant for lunch, although I was too nervous to eat much. After that, the interview lasted all afternoon. I must have talked to half a dozen different people. At this point it all blurs together."

"It must have been megastressful," Diane said, opening the trunk of her car to load Beverly's luggage. "What kind of questions did they ask? It's been ages since I've had a job interview."

"What didn't they ask? They questioned everything I put on my résumé. I think my job qualifications passed with flying colors, but they seemed to have some reservations about whether I would be happy relocating. At least, they talked about it quite a bit," Beverly said.

"Would you be comfortable leaving your father?" Diane asked.

"That's the big question, but I don't have to make that decision until they offer me the position. In fact, I'm so tired of plane hopping and talking about myself, the only thing I want to do is sleep for twenty-four hours. I hardly got a wink last night. I was too wound up to relax."

"I can understand why. Feel free to sleep on the way back to Marble Cove."

"Thanks, but I rarely sleep in cars or planes." Beverly's mind flashed back to the fateful train ride where she'd narrowly escaped death. If she'd been asleep in her original seat, she wouldn't be alive today.

Diane seemed to sense she didn't want to talk about a new job, and Beverly was grateful for her restraint. The truth was, she was tremendously excited about working in the private sector again. Even though she was telecommuting full time and building up her consulting business on the side, she missed the interaction with people in a conventional work environment. The people at the pharmaceutical company seemed to love what they were doing, and they made her eager to get a fast-track job. There was tremendous potential if they offered her the position.

The world outside the car windows seemed especially gray and unappealing today. The remaining snowdrifts were gritty from dirt carried by the strong March winds. The trees they passed were mostly scraggly evergreens, not showing any new spring growth. Would she be as willing to leave the Maine coast in summer when the ocean lapped the sun-bleached beach she loved? Or in the fall when the woods burst into flame-colored glory?

"Won't it be nice when spring finally gets here?" she asked, realizing how long she'd been lost in her own thoughts.

Diane mumbled assent, obviously daydreaming too.

Beverly wasn't ready to say more about her interview, not even to Diane. It was difficult to weigh what she'd lose against what she could gain in the new job. In the short time she'd been back living with her father, she'd made some close friends. It would be hard to leave them and the support they so willingly offered.

There are potential friends everywhere, she told herself, but she might never meet three women like Diane, Margaret, and Shelley. They had a depth of understanding that made their friendship precious.

Diane dropped her off at her father's house but declined to come in.

"I keep hoping Rocky will be waiting on my doorstep when I get home," she said. "I can't believe he's a runaway. There must be something keeping him away. But then, I've always been something of an optimist."

After thanking Diane again, Beverly went inside. Her father was napping in his favorite chair, and she tried to tiptoe up the stairs to her room without waking him. She didn't count on Mrs. Peabody waylaying her before she could reach the third step.

"Welcome home! Did you have a good time?"

Beverly and her father had decided not to say anything to Mrs. Peabody about her job interview. Much as she liked and relied on the elderly woman, Beverly knew how much she loved to gossip. There would be plenty of time to tell her—and announce it to the whole town—if she was offered the job and decided to take it.

"I didn't expect you to be here this afternoon," Beverly said.

"It's such a cold, nasty day, I thought soup would go over well. I just came by to add noodles to the Crock-Pot. The secret of my soup is putting in the ingredients at just the right time," Mrs. Peabody said.

"You do make delicious soup," Beverly said, continuing up the stairs before Mrs. Peabody could overwhelm her with a barrage of questions.

When she came back downstairs half an hour later, Mrs. Peabody was gone, and her father was puttering in the kitchen, making himself a cup of tea.

"I didn't hear you come in," he said. "Want a cup of Earl Grey?"

"Please. You were sleeping in your chair. I didn't see any reason to wake you."

"Best sleep I get all day. Maybe I should spend the night in my recliner."

"You know you'd get a stiff neck if you did that," she said in a teasing voice, waiting for him to ask about her trip.

She didn't have long to wait.

"Well, how did you like Chicago?" he asked, sitting down at the table to sip his hot drink.

"I only saw it through the windows of a taxi."

"Cities are getting too big," he said, revisiting a favorite topic of his. "I wouldn't live there if they deeded me the city."

"A place like Chicago has its big business and cultural center, but people live in a collection of neighborhoods, each with its own particular flavor. The plant where I'd be working is actually in a suburb north of the city," Beverly said.

"Don't tell me the suburbs are just like Marble Cove, only bigger," he said with a skeptical snort.

"Well, there is Lake Michigan. It's not the ocean, but you can't see across it."

He snorted again. "What about the job?"

"It sounds interesting, but they haven't offered it to me yet."

"And if they do?"

"I haven't decided."

"Well, do what you think is best for you. I'd miss you, but I get along fine on my own."

Beverly stooped and kissed the top of her father's balding head. Part of the reason she loved him so much was because he'd always supported whatever she wanted to do. Both of her parents had raised her to believe she could do whatever she put her mind to. Although she still missed her mother nearly five years after her death, she was immensely grateful for her father. The biggest question about taking a job in Chicago was whether she should—or could—leave him. He loved his books and his quiet life, but he seemed more frail with each passing year. Did she want to be far away if he needed her? He wouldn't have any patience with that dilemma, but it was foremost in her mind when she thought of moving away.

Her father always went to bed several hours before Beverly felt sleepy enough to do the same. Although she was physically exhausted from the whirlwind trip, she was still too keyed up to consider going to bed as early as he did. Instead she took her laptop computer to her room and settled down on her bed with a mound of pillows behind her back to check her e-mail.

She gave hurried answers to a few inconsequential messages but saved the most interesting one for last. Jeff Mackenzie kept in contact with Beverly as he traveled on assignments. He was an excellent photographer who worked all over the world, and his messages to her always came with interesting photos and commentaries. This week he was in Mexico doing a spread for a travel magazine.

"I tried to get a series on a pyramid without any tourists in the scene, but it seems everyone in the world wants their picture taken," he'd written.

Beverly smiled at his descriptions and wondered what it would be like to be in a different place every few days. Jeff made it sound exciting, but she also suspected he got tired of hotel rooms and restaurant food.

The last picture he posted showed him in khaki shorts and shirt with camera equipment hanging from his shoulder. She stared at his photo for several minutes, wondering whether their fledgling relationship would go anywhere. He was conventionally handsome, tall and dark haired with a warm smile. When he wore sunglasses and a hat, he looked like a version of Indiana Jones, but he was very much his own man. He worked freelance and was comfortable enough financially to pick and choose the assignments he wanted.

Would she see more or less of him if she moved to Chicago? Should she consider her feelings for him when she decided whether to make the change? Like everything else in her life lately, it was a decision she couldn't make right now. She decided it would be better to tell him about her job interview in person, although she wasn't sure when she would see him again. She hoped it wouldn't be too long. He made a point of stopping in Marble Cove to see her whenever he was in the state.

She put aside the computer without sending Jeff a reply, closed her eyes tight and tried to think of her response if she was offered the job.

After several minutes, she felt relaxed enough to turn out the light and pull the covers up under her chin. The activity of the last two days caught up with her, and she fell into a deep sleep.

In the morning when she unpacked her travel case, she found a restaurant menu she'd secreted away. It was a list of the desserts at the fancy French restaurant where she'd had lunch, and she'd immediately thought of Shelley when she saw it. There were pastries, cakes, and fruit delicacies she'd never tried, including some she'd never heard of. She thought her friend might get a kick out of seeing it.

After breakfast and a lengthy conversation with Mrs. Peabody about whether to make a tuna noodle casserole, which her father disliked, Beverly decided to walk to the Bauers' house. For the first time in what seemed like ages, the sun was shining brightly, chasing away the drab gray vista outside her door.

"Come in," Shelley said with a welcoming smile. "You're just in time to try a butterscotch walnut cookie."

"Only a taste," Beverly said. "I just finished breakfast."

She followed Shelley to the new kitchen, a delightful room with big windows to let in lots of light.

"This is my temporary helper, Tami Harper," Shelley said, introducing a tiny redhead with flour up to her elbows. "She's staying with her mother during her break from culinary school."

"I don't want to interfere with your work," Beverly said. "I picked up a dessert list from a French restaurant in suburban Chicago. I thought you might like to see it."

It was Tami, not Shelley, who avidly reached for the fancy little folder.

"Oh my, look at this," she said without giving Shelley a chance to see it. "Café au lait crème tarts. I've always wanted to try making them. The secret is in the real cream. Watery half-and-half won't do it."

Beverly gave Shelley a puzzled look, not sure exactly what Tami was doing there. Her friend shook her head and waited patiently until her helper passed the list to her.

"They're too fancy for my clientele," she said, "but I really appreciate your bringing it. I like to collect dessert menus when I can get them. Here, I just put this batch on the cooling rack. Please help yourself."

Tami excused herself. "It was nice to meet you, Beverly. I have to get started on my white chocolate macadamia nut glaze. It's for a birthday cake that has to be delivered this afternoon."

Beverly took a warm cookie to be polite, but she was much more interested in Shelley's helper. Macadamia glazes didn't sound at all like the kind of baking her friend usually did.

"I have to go," Beverly said. "I have a few errands to run, and it's nice to have a sunny day to do it."

"Mama!" Aiden's bright voice was too loud to ignore, and Shelley quickly thanked Beverly for stopping by.

"Isn't Adelaide here today?" Beverly asked.

"She was here earlier, but I think Allan took her to the community center. Aiden's had a little tummy ache, and when he doesn't feel well, he always wants his mother's attention. I don't understand why he's been getting them lately, but I guess it's his age. I'd better see to him."

"Nice to meet you, Tami," Beverly said before she let herself out, a bit puzzled by what was going on in her friend's kitchen.

Home businesses were no snap, she decided. Was that one more indication she should go back into the workforce instead of trying to make a living on the computer from her home?

Her next stop was the library to pick up a book her father had on reserve. She'd just left with the book tucked in the crook of her arm when she saw a familiar face coming toward her.

Beverly hadn't seen Dennis Calder in a couple of weeks, although he had a condo in one of the town's newer areas, Sunrise Shores, and looked in on his grandfather, Albert Calder, from time to time. The elder Calder was her father's archenemy, if squabbling over trivial matters in the neighborhood deserved such a dramatic label.

"Beverly Wheeland, I had a feeling this was going to be a good day when I saw the sun shining. You look terrific!"

"Hello, Dennis." She wasn't quite sure how to respond to his overblown compliment.

"I'm on my way to the library to check their copy of the *Wall Street Journal*. For some reason, I haven't gotten mine yet this week. Do you have time for a cup of coffee?"

"Sounds nice, but I have to get home with this book. My father will be on pins and needles until he gets his hands on it."

"Sounds like my grandfather," he said with a laugh. "There's a small branch hanging down on the tree in his front yard. If I don't trim it off pretty soon, he's going to have a fit."

"It hasn't been good weather for tree trimming," she said.

"No, I don't like the idea of being up on a ladder when the wind is blowing hard, but my grandfather thinks my generation is soft. I guess I'll have to take care of the limb today just to show him I can do it."

"Well, good luck." Beverly started to walk away, but Dennis fell into step beside her.

"If you don't have time now, how about this evening? Have dinner with me, and we can catch up on each other's news."

"That sounds nice," she said diplomatically, "but I really can't do it. Thanks for asking." She had to give him points for persistence.

"Maybe another time." He fell back while she hurried toward her father's house.

She gave the book to her father and was rewarded by his happy smile. Given the way he felt about Albert Calder, she definitely wasn't going to mention seeing his grandson. Beverly started to go to her room but instead stood at the bottom of the steps gazing out the window. The smaller branches of the bare old oak in the yard were whipping wildly in the March gusts, and she couldn't help but think of her own jumbled emotions about the winds of change blowing through her life. Was she ready to move on, or would she regret leaving Marble Cove and her father behind if opportunity presented itself?

It came to her then what the real question was. What did she really want from life?

Chapter Ten

Adelaide was all smiles when she arrived at Shelley's house Thursday morning. She proudly opened a cloth bag woven in earth tones and took out a plastic pig.

"What do you have there?" Shelley asked, holding Emma on one hip.

"My piggy bank. I bought it with my pay." Adelaide rattled it to show it contained some coins. "Don't you think it's cute?"

"Yes, it certainly is," Shelley said, tweaking the curly tail.

Adelaide held out a small red coin purse with a zipper. "I put my money to spend here. Dad takes me to the Mercantile when he goes. They have lots of good things."

She tucked the purse into one of the deep pockets in her coat before hanging it up.

"It's a good idea to keep it in your coat pocket so the children don't find it," Shelley said, happy Margaret and Allan were allowing her to pay a small salary for Adelaide's help. "I'm so glad you're here. I haven't had time to dress Emma, and Tami is already in the kitchen."

"Can I help with cookies today?" Adelaide asked.

"I'd love to have you, but Tami is helping me in the kitchen today."

Adelaide looked crestfallen.

"I don't have enough jobs there for both of you, but it's much more important to watch the children. Is that okay? Emma's pink overalls are in a laundry basket with other clean clothes. It's in our bedroom."

Adelaide's face brightened. "Okay," she said.

In her morning prayers, Shelley had given thanks for Adelaide's help and the love her children had for her. She honestly didn't know what she'd do without her. Her business was starting to show a fair profit, but with Dan out of work, money was much too tight to put the children in day care.

"I have something to show you," Tami said, waving a book as she burst out of the kitchen. "Oh, good morning, Adelaide. It's good you could come this morning. Shelley and I have so many things to bake."

"I'll be right there after I get the kids settled in with Adelaide," Shelley told Tami before she headed up the stairs. She took time to talk with Aiden in his room for a few minutes while Adelaide went to find a clean outfit for his sister.

"You'll be good, won't you?" she asked. Her son was sweet and cooperative ninety percent of the time, but it distressed Adelaide when he lost his temper.

"I left my very best cars at Meemaw's house. I want Daddy to get them for me."

"Daddy has other things to do this morning. I did tell you not to take them with you. Remember?"

He sent a toy truck racing across his bedroom floor until it disappeared under his bed. "I want my cars."

"Meemaw will save them for you. Now be good, or you'll have to sit on a stool and watch me work."

"Can I have a cookie?"

"*May* I," Shelley corrected, "but not now. Maybe for lunch."

"Then can Jeremy come over?"

"Not today. He's in day care," Shelley reminded him. "Maybe he can come Saturday."

She left him playing on the floor and hoped he would be reasonably content. Making him sit on a stool, even for a few minutes, was more punishment for her than for him. She had enough to cope with.

"I'm so excited about this order," Tami said when Shelley went into the kitchen. "Twenty dozen finger treats, and we can choose what to make."

"Oh, you have the slip for the Garden Club fund-raiser. My friend Margaret is a member. She recommended me, so I want to give them a good selection. Nothing too fancy though. They put the emphasis on auctioning off flower arrangements and donated items. The punch and cookies don't take center stage."

"But what a wonderful opportunity to showcase what we can do," Tami said. "I've been looking in your books, and I've found a wonderful recipe for lemon curd tarts. You can decorate them with edible flowers so they'll match the theme of the evening. All the best pastry chefs are using them now."

"Oh dear." Shelley was bowled over by her helper's extravagant idea. "I'd have to order the flowers way ahead from an out-of-town source, and it would be expensive. The Garden Club has a pretty tight budget. They're trying to raise money for plants to beautify the town."

"Well, edible flowers are out then," Tami said in a disappointed voice. "I guess ordinary tarts would be okay. In New York, they'd... Of course, you know the tastes of your customers."

Shelley understood that Tami wanted to try the fancy recipes she'd learned in culinary school, but she was planning to make bars and cookies. If she kept things simple, she could fill the order with delicious finger treats and still make a reasonable profit.

"I was thinking lemon bars," she said. "Macaroons are always popular, and of course, we'll need something chocolate."

"If you're doing bars, I know a wonderful recipe I got from my grandmother for date-nut bars. They use whipped egg whites and pecans along with chopped dates," Tami said. "They'd be a little out of the ordinary."

Shelley tried to remember what dates and pecans had cost the last time she bought them. She wasn't stingy about her ingredients, but the Garden Club event didn't call for expensive gourmet treats.

"I didn't plan to shop for more ingredients," she said thoughtfully. "I'm pretty well stocked up already. Tell you what, why don't you come up with something—not tarts—

using what I have on hand. I'll let you do your own thing and count on you for about three dozen of something."

"Great. I'll get right on something special, to jazz up the offerings."

"Not too special," Shelley warned, although she suspected Tami only heard what she wanted to hear.

Fortunately she'd had the foresight to freeze a supply of chocolate chip oatmeal cookies, a favorite with almost everyone who ordered from her. She also had a large container of spritz cookies with dabs of chocolate and strawberry icing in the centers. They always looked especially nice on a platter covered with a cut-paper doily. If Tami's cookies were nice enough to send to the Garden Club—and they probably would be—she was in pretty good shape on that order.

"When will you need the oven?" she asked her helper.

"I'll be ready for it around nine thirty."

Shelley calculated how long it would take to get her lemon bars ready to bake and realized they both needed to start baking at the same time.

"I need it then too," she said.

"Do you want to know how we learned to schedule oven use at my school?" Tami asked, then went on to tell her without waiting for a reply. "My instructor taught us to write everything down. He kept a note pad near the oven. If more than one person had to use the oven, we signed up, putting a beginning and end time along with the temperature needed. It saved a whole lot of waiting and arguing about whose turn it was. It works so well, I use it even when I'm baking by myself. That way, I always have the oven at exactly the right temperature at the right time."

Shelley had to admit it sounded like a good idea. She was always waiting for an oven to heat up or cool down to a lower temp. Maybe Dan could install a small magnetic board to hold a daily schedule. Meanwhile, she went to check on the kids and found a small notepad to use as Tami had suggested. She'd never been big on writing things down, but while she had a helper, it made good sense.

"I have it!" Tami said looking up from the computer. *"Tartelettes de framboises au mascarpone."*

"Tartelettes…" That was as far as Shelley could get before the French pronunciation tripped her up.

"Raspberry tarts," Tami giggled. "I would need a few frozen raspberries and some pistachio nuts, but I can run to the store and get them."

What part of *using the ingredients on hand* hadn't Tami understood? Shelley took a deep breath. "No, too fancy," she firmly insisted.

"You don't need to be afraid of French pastry," Tami said stiffly. "It's really not that difficult. The secret is mixing by hand. You have to work fast so the butter doesn't get soft. If you over mix in a food processor, the pastry won't turn out the way it should." Tami made fluttery movements with her hands to make her point.

"I'm sure it would be delicious, but it's too elaborate for the Garden Club order."

"Well, if you want something more ordinary, I could make French pastry shells and fill them just before you start serving. I could give people a choice of fillings and complete them at the table. Something fun," Tami said.

"No, I don't think so," Shelley said, feeling unsophisticated in light of Tami's suggestions.

"Mama!" Emma burst into the kitchen followed by Adelaide.

"Oh, you sweet little darling," Tami said, scooping up the toddler and kissing her cheek.

"She has a boo-boo," Adelaide announced.

"Let me see," Shelley said, taking her and setting her on an open patch of counter to examine the finger she held out. "No blood."

"She pinched it on one of Aiden's cars," Adelaide explained.

"Let Mama kiss it," Shelley said. "There, all better."

Pacified by the attention, Emma was content to leave the kitchen with Adelaide. Somewhat to Shelley's surprise, Tami went down on one knee and waved good-bye.

"She's such a doll," Tami said.

Her bars and cookies must seem terribly dull to a nearly-trained pastry chef, but Shelley was adamant about keeping things simple. "Let's get back to work," she said. "Just use ingredients I have on hand, and whatever you make has to go on a plate with the bars and cookies."

She went to work on her lemon bars, a favorite with many of her customers. They gave just the right amount of tart and sweet, and Margaret would be pleased to have them included in her club's order.

Although she was curious about what Tami was doing, Shelley tried not to oversee her activity. She'd given her helper the responsibility for three dozen treats. Now she had to give her the freedom to do the job. It wasn't easy being a boss, but Shelley reminded herself it was only temporary.

Tami liked to chat while she worked, and Shelley didn't discourage her, even though the constant flow of words was distracting. Somewhat to her surprise, the written oven schedule did make the baking process go more smoothly. Tami was taking pans of cone-shaped pastries out just in time for Shelley to put the lemon bars in to bake.

Shelley watched Tami take her cooled filling out of the fridge, then started washing her own bowls and utensils. Shelley made it a point to clean up after each batch, and this time she did Tami's too. Although her helper was willing to do any kitchen chores, she tended to leave her used equipment all over the place. She wasn't big on soaking either, so Shelley had to scrub hard to clean off dried dough.

She sighed softly and wondered whether she should check on the children. Adelaide was totally trustworthy, but her motherly instincts kicked in when things were too quiet. When the dishes were clean, she left the kitchen to see what was up.

The doorbell rang, and Aiden came barreling out of his room to answer it.

"Meemaw!" he cried out when he opened the door.

"How's my little sweetie?" Frances Bauer asked, hugging Aiden with one hand and holding a canvas bag in the other.

"Did you bring my cars?" he asked, always one to get right to the point.

"Hello, Shelley," Frances said. "Fortunately I needed to go downtown anyway when Aiden called me about his cars. He's getting good at dialing my number, isn't he?"

"He's supposed to ask first," Shelley said, giving her son a look that promised they would talk later.

"Where's my baby granddaughter?" Frances asked.

"Playing baby stuff with Adelaide," Aiden said. "Can I have my cars now?"

"*May* I please have my cars," his grandmother corrected him.

"You really didn't have to make a special trip for toy cars," Shelley said.

"It's no trouble for my special boy."

Shelley took a deep breath and decided to let the matter drop for now. Her relationship with Dan's mother had gone through shaky times, especially since at first she seemed to blame Shelley for Dan's shortcomings. But Shelley had recently come to appreciate Frances more as a source of support and knew that deep down she was a good person.

Adelaide came out holding Emma's hand as she toddled toward her grandmother. Frances handed the bag to Aiden so he could retrieve his cars and hurried to scoop up the baby.

"Here's my precious darling. Are you being a good little girl?"

Emma squirmed in her arms. Being grabbed and hugged was a little overpowering, and she scampered back to Adelaide when Frances released her.

"I smell something good," the older woman said, taking Aiden by the hand. "Let's go see what Mommy is making."

Shelley followed her mother-in-law to the kitchen where Tami was finishing her miniature crème horns.

"What do we have here?" her mother-in-law asked Tami. "Aren't they adorable! Is that a vanilla filling?"

"No, it's green tea–ginger crème, not as sweet as a regular pudding or marshmallow filling. According to the teachers at my school, there's a trend in upscale restaurants to play down extreme sweetness in favor of a more sophisticated flavor. I've made extra, so feel free to try one if you like."

"If you don't mind." Frances picked up one of the delicate pastry horns and took a small bite. "I'm amazed. It's absolutely delicious. It's so nice to see gourmet desserts coming out of your new kitchen, Shelley."

Shelley looked with dismay at the tiny little pastry horns. They were cute and, if Frances was to be believed, delicious, but they were so small she felt obligated to add extra to the Garden Club order. She planned to have each item be a substantial treat, but Tami's were hardly a bite.

"Would you like to try one?" Tami asked, basking in Frances's praise.

"Can I have a cookie?" Aiden asked, coming into the kitchen.

"Not until lunch," Shelley told him for the second time. "You know you've been having tummyaches lately."

"One little cookie can't hurt," his grandmother said, going over to the ceramic cookie jar where Shelley kept a few cookies for her family. She handed him a big chocolate chip cookie, and he eagerly bit into it.

Frances beamed at his enthusiasm. When she smiled, she looked a little like her handsome son, although frown lines were beginning to etch her forehead and the lines beside her mouth. She was still wearing her fleece-lined tan suede coat, and the heat in the kitchen brought a pink flush to her usually pale cheeks.

"Would you like to take your coat off?" Shelley asked.

"No, thank you, Shelley. I'll be running along as soon as I see what's in your oven. Is it something else Tami made?"

"No, there are lemon bars almost ready to come out, and I made them."

"Oh yes, you brought some for Sunday dinner one time. Was that Thanksgiving or Dan's birthday?"

"Neither," Shelley said, quickly changing the subject so she didn't have to debate when she'd last made them for a family dinner. "Are you going to the Garden Club fund-raiser?"

"I'd like to, but I'm hosting my bridge club that night. I may call the members and ask if they'd mind rescheduling."

Shelley saw her out, but not before she warned Aiden not to get the chocolate she'd given him on her jacket.

Back in the kitchen, she washed her son's face and hands, then hurried to take out the lemon bars. Tami was watching her expectantly, and she knew she should try one of the little horns and tell her it was good.

"Will they freeze all right?" she asked, biting into a disappointingly bland horn.

"I'm sure they will."

"They'll look nice on the dessert platters," Shelley said.

It was true. Tami's creations made hers look bulky and old-fashioned, even though she was sure hers tasted better. The horns were delicate and skillfully executed, and she doubted whether she would ever be able to make such artful pastries. Was she in the wrong business?

CHAPTER ELEVEN

Margaret shivered in spite of her warm coat and the long blue and green striped scarf around her neck. Friday was still windy and cold, but at least the sun was shining. She took it as a good sign for beginning a new exercise program.

She'd elected to walk to the community center, following Beverly's advice to check out the daily programs there, as they were the best winter exercise option in Marble Cove. She could join any one of several held each morning for a nominal fee. If she didn't like one, she could try others since it wasn't necessary to sign up.

Walking rapidly to get out of the cold as soon as possible, she nearly missed seeing Diane nailing something on a telephone pole.

"Good morning, Margaret," her friend called out. "You're out early."

"I've talked myself into trying an exercise class at the community center." She walked over to see what Diane was putting on the pole. "Rocky is still missing?"

"I'm afraid so. Do you think people can recognize him from this picture? I made the posters myself, but my printer isn't as sharp as I'd like."

Margaret studied the notice for a few moments and nodded approval.

"The yellow Labrador/golden retriever mix is fairly unusual, I would think. The picture doesn't show how beautiful his coat is, but it's certainly good enough to identify him."

"That's what I think." Diane finished nailing the sign. "I've put the outdoor ones in plastic page protectors in case in rains before he's found."

"Good idea. You can count on some kind of precipitation this time of year. I hope someone spots him soon. You must be worried sick."

"I am. It's not like him to disappear—or maybe I don't know him as well as I thought. When I found him injured by a tidal pool, I thought he'd been abandoned. Maybe I was wrong. He might have a history as a runaway I know nothing about."

"He seemed so happy with you," Margaret said to console her friend.

"I thought so too, which worries me even more. I'm afraid he might be hurt somewhere, maybe hit by a car and lying along the road. Leo Spangler is keeping an eye out in case someone brings Rocky to his office, but so far all he's been able to offer is sympathy."

"Well, your poster is good. Everyone in town should be on the lookout for him now. Would you like me to post one in the community center? A lot of people would see it there. And I'll put one on the door of my gallery. We're not busy this time of year, but there's always some foot traffic on the street."

"I'd really appreciate it," Diane said as she took two posters from the canvas bag on her shoulder. "I'm going to post one on the bulletin board at the grocery store and any other place where I can get permission."

"Most of the stores won't be open yet."

"I know, but I'll come back later. I can't concentrate on writing when Rocky could be in all sorts of trouble."

"I hope you find him soon," Margaret said. "I know how much Rocky means to you. Our cats are precious to us. Adelaide was devastated when Oreo went missing. Fortunately, we got her kitty back."

"Yes, people do get attached to their pets. I never realized how much until I adopted Rocky."

"Well, good luck finding him. I'd better get going. I don't want to be late for my first class."

"I'll walk a block with you. What class are you taking?"

"I wish I knew. There's a list posted on the bulletin board. I'll just read through it and pick whatever sounds the most like me."

"Hope you enjoy your exercise," Diane said when they parted company.

Margaret was sorry to lose Diane's companionship, and she wasn't looking forward to her foray into the community center's program. She'd never enjoyed group exercise, preferring a solitary walk or a bracing swim in the ocean, but her health scare made it seem mandatory she do something else during the long winters.

When she got to the buff brick building housing the community center, she took her time hanging her coat on a rack in the corridor. Several women had just arrived looking rather chic in spandex tights and thick socks. Margaret didn't own anything remotely resembling an exercise outfit, and she felt rather dumpy in her gray sweatpants and faded blue sweatshirt.

She posted Diane's notice on the edge of the bulletin board and studied the list of the center's offerings. They all had fancy names, none of which meant anything to her. The more she read, the more she wondered whether she'd be better off taking a dip in the icy waters of the Atlantic.

A variety of classes on everything from exercise to art were offered for everyone from seniors to preschoolers. She considered joining a session for seniors, but while she was deciding an elderly lady from church came up to her.

"Good morning, Margaret."

Mrs. Squires was so old no one called her by her first name. Margaret didn't even know what it was, although the octogenarian had been a resident of Marble Cove practically forever.

"Mrs. Squires, are you here for a class?"

"Yes, I never miss a session of the senior classes. It gets the blood pumping and works out the kinks. And at my age, there are plenty of kinks. You're welcome to join us, you know." She looked at the bold-faced watch she was wearing.

"Class starts pretty soon. Our leader doesn't like us to miss the warm-up."

Margaret watched the elderly lady hurry off in baggy black tights and a sleeveless sweatshirt that hung to the tops of her legs. Her legs looked thin as sticks above boxy white running shoes, but Margaret admired her for joining a class at her age.

She turned her attention back to the list of class offerings. Certainly she was too young for the session Mrs. Squires suggested, and she automatically eliminated charm school for preschoolers, although it was rather a sweet idea. She could see Shelley's little girl a few years from now in a frilly dress learning table manners and perhaps dancing with boys in bow ties. It was a lovely concept, and it never hurt to learn good manners early.

Unfortunately, she was only procrastinating by reading about classes totally unrelated to her reason for being there.

"Why, hello," Penny Tyler said, coming up behind Margaret and startling her. "I didn't think Adelaide was on the schedule to volunteer today."

Penny looked younger than her age with an unlined face and a ready smile. She did a great job as director of the special-needs program, and Margaret admired her dedication. Thanks to her, Adelaide always felt welcome at the community center. Penny was a genius at finding jobs to make her daughter feel genuinely useful and accepted.

"She's not with me today," Margaret said, happy to turn her attention away from the puzzling array of choices. "I'm here to find an exercise class. I had a bit of a health scare earlier, and I really need to find a good winter activity."

Penny smiled sympathetically. "Do you see something that appeals to you?"

Because Margaret was very fond of Penny, she bit her tongue instead of telling the program director the truth: she was overwhelmed with the choice of exercise options and would rather go home, munch on cookies, and sip a cup of tea. But Margaret knew a sedentary life wouldn't help her health or prolong her longevity.

"I'm feeling fine but a bit housebound. I need to find an exercise class to join until I can get outside. I get enough activity in the summer when I can swim in the ocean, walk, and work in my garden. What I need is something to hold me over until good weather returns."

"You won't want to swim outside until at least June," Penny said. "I'm sure we have a program that's just right for you. Have you thought of the SeniorClass? The members have a lot of enthusiasm."

Margaret didn't want to debate with the center's director, but she certainly wasn't old enough for a group with octogenarians.

"My friend Beverly Wheeland gave me some suggestions. I think this one may fill the bill." Margaret pointed randomly to one promising to shake off calories as the participants moved to the beat of lively music.

Penny laughed. "Well, good luck. You'll get a good workout in that one. I need to get back to work. Say hello to Adelaide for me. She's such a pleasure to have around."

Margaret couldn't help but feel proud of her daughter. She was the joy of her life and Allan's. Margaret was here as much for Adelaide as for herself. She wanted to be alive and healthy for her daughter as long as possible, knowing it was uncertain whether she could live on her own without one or both parents. With renewed determination, Margaret noted the time of the class combining aerobic exercise with "simple" dance moves. The description made it sound like fun. Taking a copy of the handout, she went to the center's main desk to pay the small fee for her first class.

"You're just in time," the volunteer at the desk told her. "The class starts in five minutes. You can leave your purse and coat in a locker and hang the key around your neck during the class. Mandy Scott is the instructor. I guarantee you'll get a good workout with her."

Was that a good review or a warning? Margaret hurried to the locker room and stuffed her belongings into a narrow metal closet. It reminded her of junior high gym class, not one of her fondest memories.

She passed by the open door where the SeniorClass members were sitting on the floor leaning forward and hanging onto their feet. One man in the back row sat in front of her in church. He was ninety if he was a day. She hoped they could all get up again, but she didn't have time to think about it. The room she wanted was farther down the corridor.

Margaret looked around the room where "Shake It Up and Off" was about to begin. She didn't see a soul she knew by name—which was unusual considering how long she'd lived in the small town of Marble Cove. She did recognize some familiar faces, mostly younger women, but noted in dismay she was the oldest person in the room. Resolutely, she vowed not to let that deter her. She certainly wasn't ready for the group of gray hairs, though her hair color fit the description. If the sixties were the new forties, as women's magazines liked to claim, she was at an awkward age at sixty-eight, not quite a senior citizen but no spring chick either.

Her musings on middle-age-plus were interrupted by the cheerful voice of a slender black-haired woman who'd just entered the room. Immediately the class members, who had been milling about, darted to different positions in the room.

"Excuse me." A harried younger woman wearing a pink sweatshirt stained with what looked like strained squash gestured at the polished wooden floor where Margaret was standing. "You're in my spot."

Margaret hadn't realized there were "assigned" spots, but she moved over so the woman could plant herself. She hoped she wasn't invading someone else's territory.

A few latecomers rushed in as the instructor, who introduced herself as Mandy, adjusted the volume on the CD player built into the wall and took a stance in front of them, her muscular but slim legs spread wide and hands on her hips. Everyone immediately fell silent and imitated her.

"Now make sure you work at your own pace," she instructed the class over the pulsating music.

Margaret concentrated on doing exactly as the instructor did, although it was immediately obvious she couldn't put her hands flat on the floor. Mandy led the all-women class through a series of stretches and bends as Margaret discovered muscles she'd forgotten she had.

The volume and the speed of the music picked up even more as the next song came on, and Margaret was feeling a little breathless.

Work at your own pace, she reminded herself. It was easier said than done when everyone was picking up the pace and making it look easy.

"Grapevine," Mandy shouted as the class of about twenty started to do a sidestep across the polished floor.

It took a moment for Margaret to figure out what they were doing, partly because she stopped to wipe the perspiration off her forehead with the sleeve of her sweatshirt. Obviously she was overdressed. All the young things were wearing tank tops or short-sleeved T-shirts with shorts or tights. She struggled to keep up as Mandy continued to yell out directions, but no way would her feet move as fast as the young blonde with chopped-off hair beside her.

"Cancan, cuz you know you can!" the pony-tailed instructor drilled as the women kicked their way across the floor.

Margaret felt very unkind as she noted with satisfaction the only woman having trouble keeping up, besides her, was the territorial one in the stained pink sweatshirt.

"Oh, I'm sorry," Margaret apologized as she bumped into someone next to her when the line suddenly switched from left to right.

"That's fine," the woman said, not missing a beat. "It takes awhile to catch on to all the routines, but it's a fabulous workout. You can burn up to five hundred calories an hour if you move fast enough."

Margaret wasn't sure her body could move fast enough to burn that many calories, and her brain certainly couldn't follow the complicated routines. The woman beside her was softly counting. Maybe that was the secret dancers used to stay in step. She tried for a few seconds, but the message didn't get from her head to her feet.

The instructor drilled them through exercise dance moves set to music Margaret remembered from her high school days and some she'd never heard. A roaring twenties number left her arms flapping and her feet flailing. She only managed to slap her knees together once for every three times the rest of the class did.

When Mandy called a halt to check pulses before the cooldown, Margaret was dismayed to compare hers to the colored chart on the wall. She was barely getting her heart rate up according to where a person her age should be after exertion.

Dear God, she silently prayed, *how can that be possible after so much moving around?* Had she gotten so sluggish even her blood was on a slow track?

During the cooldown, Margaret realized she hadn't moved nearly as much as her pink-cheeked classmates.

She'd had to spend so much effort trying to keep up with the complicated moves, she hadn't gotten nearly the aerobic benefit she'd hoped for.

"Okay, class, see you next time," Mandy trilled when, at last, the hour-long session was over.

"Don't worry," the woman Margaret had bumped into said to her. "It takes about six months or so to get the routines down. And Mandy is always introducing new ones. It's so much fun."

Six months? Margaret thought, as she collected her coat and purse and headed out, one of the few who didn't head to the big open shower room. She'd be lucky if she could master all the fancy footwork in six years, she decided wearily.

Why hadn't she driven? She debated whether to call Allan to pick her up, but at least she'd get some exercise if she walked. The cold air felt good after the sweaty atmosphere in the exercise room, and she needed time to decide what to tell her husband. He'd been excited about her decision to join a class, and she hated to disappoint him. But there had to be a better way to keep in shape. She liked the idea of a good workout, but she'd spent most of the hour in a state of confusion and panic. It was only through the grace of the Lord she hadn't fallen flat on her face.

Obviously Shake It Up and Off wasn't for her.

"How'd it go, honey?" Allan asked when she came into the house.

Margaret groaned. She didn't know whether to whine, cry, or just admit defeat. She opted for the latter.

"I joined the wrong class. All the women were half my age and twice as nimble. I feel like I just spent an hour trying to go up on a down escalator."

"That bad?" he asked a bit skeptically. "Maybe you just need to catch up with the others. It was your first day."

"And my last in that class," she said decisively.

"Are you going to try something else?" he asked with a concerned frown. "You know I worry about you."

"The really old people go to the SeniorClass."

"You could try that—not that you're really *old.*"

His soothing, mellow voice was one of his best characteristics, but not even his charm would convince her to stumble through another of Mandy's classes.

She was back to square one on exercising. Was there anything an aging but not old woman could do to improve her health without embarrassing herself?

CHAPTER TWELVE

I'm leaving with the kids now," Dan called out from the front door Saturday morning. "Are you sure you don't need me to deliver your cookies to the Garden Club?"

"No, the biggest help you can be is taking Emma to your mother's and spending some quality dad-time with Aiden. What are you guys going to do?"

"We're gonna look for driftwood," Aiden excitedly told her.

"It's the warmest day we've had in a long time," Dan explained, "so I thought I might find some nice pieces to make into lamps. I think Margaret would take them on consignment if I find some good driftwood. Tourists seem to like things like that."

"You always did like to play around with electrical things," Shelley said, glad her husband was enthused about a new project. "This is a good time to look for driftwood—before the summer people come and scour the beach clean."

"Yeah, that's what I thought."

He slung a large net bag over his shoulder and picked up Emma.

"I don't need boots," Aiden said, kicking them back into the closet.

"You sure do, buddy, just like I do," Dan said, pointing at his own footwear. "We don't want to ruin our shoes in the wet sand."

Shelley helped bundle him up to her satisfaction while Dan fretted to be gone.

"If I'm not here when you get home, I'll be setting up for the big event tonight. Tami volunteered to help me, so it shouldn't take too long."

Even though she had all day to deliver and arrange her baked goods, she was getting the jitters. This was one of the biggest events she'd ever baked for, and if her items were well received, she might get to do weddings or graduations or other big occasions. So far she'd only sold small birthday cakes, mostly for kids' birthdays, but maybe someday she could take a cake decorating class and learn how to do wedding cakes. But this was all in the future. Right now she couldn't wait to get to the community center where the Garden Club had rented one of the big rooms.

"Sorry I'm late," Tami said, rushing up the walk to the front door while Shelley was still standing there.

"You're right on time. I just said good-bye to my gang."

Shelley didn't know whether it was a good idea to include Tami. There was no predicting how she would act, and it was important everything went smoothly. Or maybe she was being unfair to the young woman.

"Oh, I'm sorry I missed seeing your kids. Emma gets sweeter every day, and Aiden always has something cute to say. I borrowed my Mom's SUV so we can lay the pans out flat in the back. We'd probably have to make two trips in my little car."

"Thank you for driving. Dan took the Subaru to go hunt for driftwood with Aiden."

"Whatever for?" She unzipped a bright blue nylon jacket and started toward the kitchen.

"He wants to make some lamps."

"Clever! I used to have a friend who made them out of porcelain vases he found at flea markets and garage sales. He gave it up when he ruined a Chinese vase a friend said was worth a few thousand dollars. Now he sells stuff he finds on eBay. I liked his homemade lamps, though."

When she wasn't baking, Tami liked to chatter on nonstop. Shelley was getting used to her talkative ways, although Tami's humming still got on her nerves. She thought of saying something about it, but she didn't want to offend the person who was helping her without pay. Thanks to Tami, her freezer was full to capacity with highly saleable items.

"Shall we load up?" Tami asked, focusing all her energy on the project at hand.

Shelley had rejected the idea of using disposable platters. Instead she was taking some lovely antique plates with hand-painted flowers, a wedding gift from a childless great-aunt who wanted to see her treasures go to someone who would really appreciate them. Shelley rarely used them, but they were totally appropriate for the Garden Club event. She'd carefully wrapped them in tissue paper and boxed them to take to the community center. She and Tami would arrange the cookies and crème horns after they got there. She hoped plastic wrap wouldn't make the pastry horns soggy. She wanted to kick herself for letting Tami do whatever she wanted. The horns didn't appeal to her at all.

When they got to the community center, it was buzzing with activity. Music filled the corridor where the exercise rooms were in use, and people seemed to be going every which way. An older man with silvery gray hair offered to help unload their baked goods, but Shelley politely refused. She wouldn't be able to relax until every plastic container was safely emptied and arranged on her fancy plates.

On her first trip to the events room, she was pleased to see Margaret and several other women arranging cut flowers on one of the long tables.

"What beautiful roses," Shelley said, temporarily distracted from her job.

"Aren't they?" Margaret beamed with pleasure. "Allan drove to a greenhouse at the crack of dawn to get them. We bought a big wholesale lot of flowers to make into arrangements we can auction off. You know Angie and Sue, don't you?"

Shelley nodded at two women she knew casually.

"What else are you auctioning?" Out of the corner of her eye she saw Tami going back for a second load, but she was curious about the event.

"We have several lovely quilts, one appliquéd with flowers, one embroidered—that's an antique—and a patchwork quilt using different floral patterns," Sue said. "We've tried to keep the floral theme throughout the event."

Shelley wondered whether she should have investigated Tami's suggestion of edible flowers, but they sounded expensive and difficult to obtain. Maybe she could look into them for future use.

"I have to help carry," she said, excusing herself to the busy flower-arrangers. She had butterflies in her stomach as she thought of everything that could go wrong.

Margaret came over to the food table after Shelley and Tami had brought everything into the building. Tami snapped on plastic gloves to handle the food, and Shelley hoped she'd treat the cookies a bit more gently.

"I'm excited to see what you have in all those plastic containers," her friend admitted. "And what lovely plates! They look quite old."

"My great-aunt gave them to me," Shelley told her proudly. "She said china painting was a popular hobby at the beginning of the twentieth century. Women didn't work outside the home, and they did all sorts of creative things to keep busy."

"If I could find someone as talented as the women who did these, I'd gladly take her work on consignment in my gallery," Margaret said. "I love the deep rose and vibrant pink shades."

Shelley pulled on plastic gloves of her own and started arranging her lemon bars on a plate with bold yellow and orange flowers while Tami put her crème horns on a plate with pale blue and lavender roses. Not only did the antique plates show the treats to the best advantage, they went wonderfully well with the theme of the event.

"What's in those little pastries?" Margaret asked. "I've never seen such delicate crème horns."

"Tami made them," Shelley said, giving credit to her new assistant.

"They're filled with green tea–ginger crème," Tami explained. "Would you like to sample one?"

"I couldn't do that," Margaret said. "It wouldn't be right to eat one now."

"Of course it would," Tami urged. "They're so tiny Shelley brought extra items to compensate. Here, try one."

Margaret accepted one of the exquisite little pastries and took a tiny bite.

"My goodness, I didn't expect it to taste so exotic. It's sweet but not too much so." She took another delicate bite and finished it off. "That's a new taste experience for me," she said. "Unusual but totally delicious. What a wonderful addition to your dessert menu, Shelley."

"It's all Tami's doing."

Shelley was pleased to have something so unusual for the Garden Club, especially since her friend raved about the crème horn, but she still thought they were too small. It hurt her feelings a bit that both Frances and Margaret had raved about Tami's horns. They were so small she'd had to include a few dozen extra cookies to compensate, which stretched her budget more than she liked. She would still make a profit, but not as much as she'd hoped. It was easy for Tami to be artistic with what she baked, because she didn't have to worry about costs.

Maybe she was being a grouch, but she couldn't afford Tami's free help if she drove up the overhead.

"Come see me after you're done here," Margaret said before she wandered back to the table where the other two women were working magic in donated vases, mostly ones left from flower shop arrangements.

When Shelley was satisfied with the way her baked goods were displayed, she left Tami to cover the plates with plastic wrap and went over to Margaret.

"Have you talked to Beverly recently?" Margaret asked after drawing Shelley aside.

"No, I've hardly been out of my kitchen the past few days. Is something wrong?"

"Not from her point of view, but I'm worried we might lose her."

"Lose her?" Shelley asked in alarm. "How?"

"She had a job interview in Chicago this week. She hasn't heard yet, but there's a possibility she might move there."

"What?" Shelley asked. "She moved back to Marble Cove to take care of her father. Chicago is much farther away than Augusta, where she was working. Why would she be looking so far away?"

"I don't think she was looking. A headhunter contacted her about it."

"A headhunter?" Shelley arched one brow.

"One of those people who make their living matching people to jobs, usually prestigious or highly skilled positions."

"Well, Beverly certainly deserves that kind of job. It must be a good one to tempt her to leave Maine. I wonder whether her father will go there with her if she gets the job." The day had taken a sad turn for Shelley.

"I can't imagine he would. He has Mrs. Peabody to look after him, but she's elderly herself. I just wondered whether you'd heard anything. Last I talked to Beverly, she hadn't been offered the job yet."

"I feel awfully selfish saying so, but I really would hate to see her leave," Shelley said. "I feel like we've become such good friends."

"I feel the same way," Margaret said. "Beverly, Diane, you, and I have a special bond. If she moves away, it will feel like part of us is going with her. Oh dear, I'm being melodramatic, but you understand what I mean."

Shelley nodded her head. "I'll pray for Beverly's happiness, but I don't know whether to ask the Lord to let her stay or go. This may be a wonderful opportunity for her, but losing a friend is always upsetting."

"Yes, I feel the same way. I want what's best for her, but I certainly would miss her."

"I wonder how Diane feels about it." She glanced over at the refreshment table where Tami still seemed to be busy.

"We talked briefly yesterday. She doesn't have family living here, so it would hit her especially hard if Beverly moves to Chicago," Margaret said.

"Well, if she hasn't been offered the job yet, we can still hope," Shelley said, frowning at what Tami seemed to be doing.

"I guess we can only hope whatever happens will be best for Beverly," Margaret said with a tinge of sadness in her voice.

"You're right," Shelley agreed halfheartedly.

"How is Dan doing?" Margaret asked, changing the subject. "I wish I had some framing work for him, but I haven't ordered any new *giclées* lately. Maybe Allan will need him to help with some furniture though."

"He picks up odd jobs here and there, and he's looking for something full time," Shelley said, still unable to see what Tami was doing across the room. "He's depressed about the layoff, but he puts on a good face. I wish he would find something more challenging and interesting than working on the docks and doing odd jobs."

"I'm sure he will eventually. He certainly has a lot of talent with his hands."

"Well, I'd better finish up and get home," Shelley said. "Since I'm spending so much time baking, my housework really piles up. I have to tell you again, I don't know what we'd do without Adelaide. She adores the children and is so good with them."

"Watching them makes her feel worthwhile. And now she also gets the satisfaction of being paid and practice in managing small sums. Allan is letting her shop by herself at the Mercantile from time to time. Their stock is outdated, but tourists seem to think the store is quaint. We figured it's a good place to let her practice shopping skills."

"It's the closest thing to an old-fashioned five-and-dime I've ever seen," Shelley said, getting antsy to check on

Tami. "Well, I really have to get moving. Good luck on your auction."

Tami was still working at the refreshment table. When Shelley got closer, her jaw literally dropped. Her helper had totally rearranged all the baked goods. Nothing was the way Shelley had left it.

"You've changed everything!" Shelley was beyond upset.

"My tiny crème horns looked so lonesome on a plate by themselves. If we mix up the different types, the line should move faster. People will only need to go to one or two plates to see everything."

"My lemon bars looked lovely on the plate with yellow flowers," she protested. "I wish you hadn't done that."

"It never occurred to me you might object. See how nice they look mixed in with almond crisps and the spritz cookies?" Tami seemed genuinely puzzled by Shelley's reaction.

Shelley dug her nails into her palms and was at a loss for words. Was Tami's arrangement better than hers? Should she redo all the plates the way she'd originally had them?

Was she overreacting to Tami's changes, or was her helper doing things her way to the detriment of the business? Shelley stood staring at the table, shaken because the new arrangement did look all right, but annoyed Tami had taken it upon herself to change it.

Shelley tried to calm down. Did it really matter how the items were arranged? She had confidence her baked goods would be well received. The business would show at least a modest profit, and she hoped the Garden Club event would lead to more orders. She wasn't going to say anything else, but she wasn't happy.

"You won't need to take me home," she told Tami. "It's nice out, and I'd like to walk."

"Are you sure? I'll be glad to drop you off."

"Yes, I'm sure." She walked away to get her jacket, hurrying away from Tami before she said something she might regret.

On the way home, she walked slowly, thinking about Tami. Shelley envied her culinary education, but her style was too upscale for Marble Cove. Shelley thought seriously about asking her not to come anymore, but how ungrateful would that seem? Tami volunteered her labor, and she did make it possible to keep up with orders and fill the freezer.

Shelley had never been anyone's boss. She tried to think of mistakes she'd made in handling Tami, but only one thing was clear. It was her business, and she badly needed it to succeed, both for the profits and her own self-esteem. Tami knew a lot about baking but not much about making a profit.

It was the middle of March, the sixteenth if she remembered right. Tami would return to her school at the end of the month. If she asked her to stop coming two weeks early, she might offend her mother, who went to church with Shelley. Tami would be hurt, and nothing positive would be accomplished.

Tami would have to stay.

Shelley realized she was clenching her fists so hard they hurt. She didn't dislike Tami. She just felt put down by the younger woman's high-handedness. If people liked Tami's baking better than hers, maybe she wasn't up to creating fancy items for big events.

As she approached her house, she realized how bright the sun was. The breeze that caressed her face actually seemed warm. How could she be gloomy when the promise of spring was in the air?

The rest of her time with Tami could be a blessing or a burden, she thought. *It's up to me.*

Chapter Thirteen

Beverly's mind was reeling from the details of the job offer she'd received the day before and she couldn't fall asleep. She changed position every thirty seconds and got up twice to tuck her blankets neatly under the mattress edge because she'd managed to pull them loose in her twisting and turning.

Tomorrow was church, and she really wanted to go, but somehow she had to get more than twenty minutes sleep Saturday night.

"Maybe hot milk would help me nod off," she said, getting up for the third or fourth time and padding down to the kitchen in her fuzzy backless slippers and new quilted robe.

Moving as quietly as possible so she wouldn't wake her father, she poured milk into a saucepan and slowly heated it. When she guessed it was warm enough, she had to skim the unappetizing skin off the top before pouring it into a candy-striped mug that had once held Christmas peppermints.

It was too hot. She sat at the table, blowing gently to cool it before taking a cautious sip.

"Yuck," she said aloud, swallowing a bit more and wrinkling her nose. It was worse than Mrs. Peabody's oatmeal, but she managed to finish it by eating some vanilla wafers to take away the taste.

When she returned to her room, she still didn't feel the slightest bit sleepy. Turning on the light on the nightstand beside her bed, she rummaged around for the book she'd been reading on the flight home from Chicago. It was an unhelpful self-help book on climbing the corporate ladder and so dull she'd fallen asleep reading it. The book only reminded her of the big decision she had to make. She tossed it aside and snuggled under the covers, resigned to waiting for dawn.

Friday afternoon she'd heard from the woman who'd interviewed her. Beverly's stomach had been in knots when she identified her caller, and it still felt like the site of a butterfly convention.

They wanted her.

Not only that, they hoped she could begin work almost immediately and offered to pay for her moving expenses.

She'd expected to wait a few weeks, at least, before hearing from them. Instead they'd made their decision to hire her in only days. She was thrilled by the offer but floored by the need to give them an answer before Wednesday of next week. How could she plan such a life-altering change with only a few days to make up her mind?

When she'd told them the news, Margaret and Diane's reactions only confirmed what good friends she had in Marble Cove. They'd both understood her dilemma. She liked working with people, but wasn't completely sure that her consulting business would be successful. On the other hand, she was getting closer to her father and very much wanted to make whatever years he had left as pleasant as possible.

"Do what's best for you," he'd said several times after she told him about the offer.

She wanted the job. There was no question about that. But did she want it enough to leave her father and friends for life in a huge metropolitan area where she knew no one?

Making friends had never been a problem. She wasn't shy, and she'd enjoyed the company of co-workers in Augusta. No doubt she'd become acquainted with many new people if she went to Chicago.

And what about Jeff? Would she see him more or less if she moved to Illinois? She hadn't told him about the interview or the offer yet. It was the kind of news better delivered in person.

When her alarm rang, she realized she'd finally fallen asleep. Bleary-eyed and still in a quandary, she hurriedly showered and dressed for church in a forest green pantsuit with a beige turtleneck top.

In spite of the sunny day yesterday, the weather had turned colder and brought a dusting of snow overnight. She liked the sparkling flakes coating the tree limbs and branches, making everything look clean and fresh. She wished it were that easy to make a fresh start in life.

Mrs. Peabody didn't come on Sunday morning, which was rather a relief given Beverly's mood. Her mind was too full of the decision she had to make for idle conversation.

"Father, are you up?" she called outside the door of his room.

"Do you see me up?" His voice was muffled.

It wasn't like Father to sleep in this late, but he was the most important person when it came to considering the new job, and she wanted to talk it over with him. He pretended he was fine with whichever decision Beverly made, but was he really? Would she greatly regret leaving him if his health took a turn for the worse? Was there any possibility at all that he'd move to Chicago with her? She very much doubted it.

"Do you want breakfast before church?"

"I think I'll pass this morning. Woke up with a scratchy throat."

"Sorry to hear that. Can I get you anything?"

"No, thanks."

"Maybe we can talk more about my job offer before Mrs. Peabody comes to fix Sunday dinner," she said.

"She's not coming. Had some family thing to go to."

"We'll have a nice brunch instead. How about some egg bakes?" she asked.

"With real eggs, not that artificial stuff?"

Beverly agreed, knowing he couldn't tell the difference once the individual ramekins were flavored with mushrooms, onions, and other good things.

She was beginning to feel silly having a conversation with a door between them.

"All right, Father. I'll see you after church."

Beverly elected to walk. She needed time to organize her thoughts, and the cold March wind seemed to clear away the cobwebs in her head.

For most of her adult life, she'd been a skeptic, but her recent journey of faith added a new dimension to her life. She'd found a church home at Old First, the oldest house of worship in Marble Cove. It wasn't the exact church built by Jeremiah Thorpe's congregation, which had been made from wood and not stone. That building, built in 1775, later burned to the ground, although some good came of it. The warning light at the lighthouse went out that night in 1789, but the crew of a ship saw the burning church and were saved from wrecking on the dangerous coast. A new structure was built soon after, the foundation around which the current building was erected.

The building was a rock-solid example of neo-Gothic architecture with stunningly beautiful stained glass windows and an impressive pipe organ. Beverly took her place in one of the middle dark oak pews and let the tranquility of the church ready her spirit for worship. This morning she didn't see the urgent need for restoration throughout the old church, a pet project of hers. Instead she let the ambiance of the nave and the worshipful quiet of the congregation give her a receptive mind. The services usually gave her a feeling of peace and a deep sense of God's presence, and today she especially needed spiritual guidance.

She silently prayed for an answer to her dilemma, and tried to keep her heart open for the answer.

When Reverend Locke began his sermon, she listened avidly, hoping to hear a helpful message. When Silas Locke spoke to the congregation, he grabbed the attention of everyone, from children sitting with their parents to the elderly ladies who shared the front bench to better hear him. In the pulpit his intensity brought his message to life. It was the way Locke preached that first drew Beverly to Old First. His teaching helped make sense of matters of faith in a way she had not experienced before.

To the casual observer, he was a rather scholarly man, bald with a fringe of dark hair and a beard only lightly flecked with gray. He was always pushing his gold-rimmed glasses up on his thin nose, a nervous habit not quite in keeping with his natty dressing. When not preaching, he favored tweed jackets with elbow patches worn over a clerical collar. No one would describe him as a warm person, but there was kindness behind his stern exterior.

This was why Beverly had been so surprised and a bit hurt when he reacted so negatively over the discovery of the original bell tower, a long forgotten part of the older church. His emphatic reaction was just one more mystery in Marble Cove, a town with more than its share of puzzles.

The gospel lesson this morning was a familiar one, the calling of the disciples, but Reverend Locke used it to give a particularly powerful sermon.

"We all have to make difficult decisions at some time in our lives," he said, "but we never have to make them alone. God is with us. If we trust in Him, right answers will come."

Beverly felt as though he were speaking directly to her. At the conclusion of the service, she prayed the minister was right. She still didn't know what her answer about the job would be, but she realized she didn't have to decide alone.

After the service she skipped the coffee hour and the congenial fellowship that went with it. Her father would be hungry, and with his diabetes, it was important for him to eat at regular hours.

If she went to Chicago, who would prepare his meals at times when Mrs. Peabody wasn't there? She was supposed to be a part-time cook, not a full-time caregiver, although she did seem to enjoy looking in on "the Mister" at odd hours of the day.

Beverly tried hard to think of some way to persuade her father to move to Chicago with her, but it seemed a hopeless cause. Marble Cove had been his favorite summer destination, and although they hadn't lived there while Beverly was growing up, he'd chosen it as a retirement home. He was as active in the community as his health would allow, and she doubted any argument would persuade him to move to a large city like Chicago.

"I'm home," she called out as she entered through the front foyer. "Let me change, and I'll get started on brunch." There was no response, so she checked the study where her father spent many hours reading and checking historical facts, a passion of his after many years teaching high school social studies. He was there with his nose in a book.

"How does brunch in about an hour sound?" she asked.

"I'll just have a bowl of cereal." His voice sounded hoarse.

"You love egg bakes," she reminded him. "They don't take that long, and we have some of the sharp cheddar you love to sprinkle on top."

"Well, if it's not too much trouble."

They had to talk, but not until he had a nice brunch.

She was taking two colorful ceramic ramekins out of the oven when he came into the kitchen.

"Did you use real eggs?" he asked.

"Yes, and as a special treat, I added some bacon bits." She felt a bit deceitful because she'd used one egg and extended it with the cholesterol-free substitute, but she couldn't taste much difference and doubted her father could either.

He read the Sunday paper, going through every section page by page even though she couldn't imagine what he found of interest in classified ads or the many advertising inserts for businesses in Augusta. She suspected he just didn't want to talk about her job offer.

"Reverend Locke talked about letting God help with important decisions," she said to open the conversation they had to have.

"All well and good, but unless the good Lord comes down and whispers in your ear, you're the one who has to decide whether to take the Chicago job."

"You know I need your input."

"You've had it. If you want the job, take it. I won't stand in your way." He peered over the paper at her. "You know your mother and I always encouraged you to be successful in whatever field of business you chose. I'm not about to change that now."

"That's not the point. I don't want to leave you. We could find a nice condo together in one of the northern suburbs. They probably have great libraries in the area, and you're sure to meet some people your age. You could go to a senior center—"

"I'm not going to sit around playing bingo with a bunch of old folks. And I know what a workaholic you are. I'd be lucky to see you fifteen minutes a day. I came to Marble Cove, and I'm staying in Marble Cove, but I don't want you to pass up a good opportunity because of me. I get along fine on my own, and I have Mrs. Peabody to fix some meals," he said, then added, "even if she does talk my ear off sometimes."

"I don't feel right about leaving you."

"And I don't feel right standing in your way when you have a good job offer. Do you know how many people would give their eye teeth for a chance like that?"

Beverly picked at her fluffy egg soufflé, but her appetite had vanished. The conversation with her father was going nowhere. She didn't doubt he would miss her, but would he be all right without her? He'd suffered sporadic memory loss and confusion as a result of recently diagnosed TIAs, or a series of ministrokes. He was on medication to minimize their occurrence, but would he take pills as prescribed if she left him on his own?

"I think I'll walk over to Diane's," she said after loading the dishwasher when they'd finished eating. "Is there anything you need before I go?"

Her father had retreated to his study, his favorite room, and was reading a book on Maine history she'd found for him online.

"No, you run along." He didn't even look up from his book.

Beverly left, but her mind was uneasy.

Beverly went up to Diane's door, needing to talk to a friend although she didn't know what there was to say. Her father didn't try to convince her to stay, but she was still uncomfortable with his offhand assurances about doing well on his own.

"Beverly, am I glad to see you," Diane said with a broad smile when she opened the door.

"You might not be after we talk. I'm pretty gloomy today."

"About the job?" Diane asked as she hung up Beverly's coat.

"They offered me a position too good to turn down, but I can't bring myself to say yes."

"Oh dear, what a dilemma. I suppose you hate to leave your father after moving here to be with him. Come into the kitchen. I'll put the kettle on and we'll talk over tea, not that I have any advice you can use, but sometimes it helps to talk things out."

"It's more than leaving my father, although that's my primary worry," Beverly said as she watched Diane put water into her teakettle. "I've settled in here."

"I'm not the only one who would hate to see you leave. It would be like the Three Musketeers losing d'Artagnan."

Beverly laughed at the literary analogy, but she couldn't deny there was a bond between the four women.

"It will be a demanding job. I'll be lucky to get home for Christmas and a short visit in the summer."

"I know how that goes. I'd love to see more of my son and daughter, but they're busy with their own lives. I'd rather they make short, happy visits rather than feeling obligated to come at regular intervals."

"My father wouldn't ask. He'd do the stiff-upper-lip bit, no matter how much he missed me. And, of course, it's expensive to fly. I'll be virtually starting over, and that's not cheap. I'll need new clothes, new furniture... My pay will be very good, but it won't stretch indefinitely."

"What about the job? Will it be exciting and challenging? Is there a good possibility for advancement?" Diane asked.

"Unfortunately, the answer to all those questions is yes. I'm being dramatic when I say it's a once-in-a-lifetime opportunity, but basically, that's true."

"I know exactly what you mean. Selling my first book was a thrill, but I'm worried about failing on the second. I'm missing Rocky terribly, but I was struggling even before he disappeared," Diane said.

"You still don't have any leads on where he is?"

"None, and the longer he's missing, the less chance there is of finding him."

"I'm so wrapped up in my own dilemma, I didn't even ask about him," Beverly said apologetically, taking another sip of her hot mint tea.

"I wouldn't want to make your decision," Diane said, "but I'll hope you'll realize soon what would be best for you."

"I appreciate your support so much," Beverly said, her eyes tearing even though she prided herself on rarely crying.

She didn't spend another sleepless night, although her rest was disturbed by vivid dreams. They were forgotten as soon as she woke up, but a vaguely anxious feeling lingered throughout the morning. She wasn't going to relax until she made the phone call.

It took a few minutes to be connected to the woman who'd offered her the job. Beverly was so nervous about her answer, she'd written a little script to follow.

"I can't tell you how much I hate to turn down your offer," she said after explaining why she couldn't leave her father.

"I see."

There was a long pause, and Beverly was sure the woman on the other end was angry. She was surprised when she came back with a counteroffer.

"I told my boss you were worth more than we offered," she said. "He authorized me to offer fifteen percent more on the salary, full dental as well as medical, and six weeks' vacation and personal time. Would that help out? You could spread it out and visit your father more often."

Beverly was dumbfounded. She'd never expected them to sweeten the deal.

"I didn't turn you down to negotiate a better offer," she said when she regained her voice.

"I didn't think so, but maybe this will help with your father. Possibly you can hire a full-time caregiver with the additional salary—not that it's my decision to make."

"Can I think about it?"

"Yes, but I do need an answer soon. We'd like to have someone on board by the first of April, and you're on a very short list of prospects."

Beverly thanked her profusely and promised to get back to her as soon as possible.

When she hung up, her hands were trembling. The rest of her life was hanging in the balance, and she didn't know what to do.

CHAPTER FOURTEEN

Margaret sighed to herself as she put her coat in a locker and braced herself to try another exercise class. The Monday noon SeniorClass was specifically tailored for, though not limited to, older participants, according to the handout she'd studied after her harried attempt to keep up with a younger group.

"Are you here for the wiggle and jiggle class?" a woman with bright henna hair asked as she stowed her coat in the locker next to the one Margaret was using.

"I beg your pardon?" She closed the steel door and tried to remember the woman's name. She was vaguely familiar, but she wasn't a Garden Club member or someone who went to Margaret's church.

"That's what we regulars call this SeniorClass. I'm Donna Gaines." She stuck out a hand to Margaret. "I bought a painting at your gallery, the lighthouse scene with a dog on the beach. My husband and I love Orlean Point Light, and we're crazy about dogs. I must have a hundred dog collectibles, statues and such, so it was a perfect choice for our dining room."

"I'm glad you're enjoying it," Margaret said. "Do you come to the SeniorClass every noon?"

"Only when the weather is too bad to walk on the beach. Of course, in Maine that's about fifty percent of the time. I have to hurry. If I don't get there first, someone will take my chair in the back row. I don't like to exercise with people watching from behind me. I'll see you there."

"Chair?" Margaret asked to Donna's retreating back but didn't get an explanation.

It wasn't hard to find the right room. An oldie by Frank Sinatra wasn't quite drowning out the hum of voices. The turnout was good, but there were enough unoccupied chairs to give pause. She didn't have a clue why people were sitting, but at least she shouldn't feel lost as she had with the younger group.

"I saved you a chair," Donna Gaines called so loudly everyone stopped talking for a few moments.

Margaret self-consciously made her way to a place in the back row.

"Thanks," she said, quite satisfied to be at the back for her first class.

As soon as she sat down, she spotted another familiar face at the end of the row.

August Jackson, known to everyone in town as Augie, smiled broadly under his big white mustache and called out to her.

"Welcome to the old folks' class, Mrs. Hoskins." He winked.

Heads turned, and she felt very much on display, but Augie had a way of making people at ease.

"Glad to be here," she said.

Augie was a bald little man with tiny black-framed glasses and a cute pug nose. A retired reporter and a cookbook author, he was in his late eighties but looked younger with a relatively unlined face. He often had helped out friends with information on Marble Cove's history. Today he was wearing a red rock-band T-shirt and baggy purple sweats, a color combination in keeping with his fondness for flashy dressing, especially bright plaids.

"Got some folks out with the flu, I suspect," he said. "Or maybe blue flu."

He lightened the mood wherever he went, but Margaret wondered whether she really belonged in a class where most participants were as old as or older than Augie.

The instructor came into the room dressed in black workout tights and a bright yellow tank top clinging to a very trim midriff. She was possibly ten years younger than Margaret and definitely twenty or thirty pounds lighter.

"Are you folks ready?" she asked in a cheerful voice. "Gayle isn't feeling well, so I'm substituting for her. I'm Georgia, and I'm so happy to see all of you here. Is there anyone new who'd like to introduce himself or herself?"

"We have Margaret Hoskins with us today," Augie said. "Most of you know she owns Shearwater Gallery."

"Let's say hello to Margaret," Georgia said.

People called out "Hello, Margaret," and Margaret briefly felt as if she'd wandered into a therapy group. At least her new friend had saved a chair in the back row where people wouldn't be watching to see whether she could keep up.

"Come on, everyone. Let's begin with leg stretches," Georgia chirped, changing the music to a spirited tune from the fifties.

"This isn't too hard," Margaret whispered to the woman beside her who seemed to be making quite a production of a few simple leg lifts.

"Oh, this is just the warm-up."

In the front row, not everyone was participating. A portly man with thinning silver hair was reading a newspaper, seemingly indifferent to the class activity. In the second row, two women were whispering, their tight white curls bobbing as they ignored the instructor.

Margaret easily did the arm stretches. She was used to painting on an easel, so they weren't a challenge.

"The music is too loud," a woman in front complained.

"Turn down your hearing aid," a helpful voice called out.

"We can barely hear back here," a third person said.

Apparently the instructor was used to interruptions. She continued as though she hadn't heard them.

"Now everyone stand in back of your chair," Georgia called out.

There was a good bit of shuffling and moving of chairs as everyone complied. It gave Margaret a chance to look at the rest of the participants, and one person took her aback. Maxine Gorman was at the end of the second row wearing bright red leotards and a yellow T-shirt two sizes too big.

She'd recently had a cake during the fellowship time after church services to celebrate her ninety-fifth birthday.

Margaret studied the face of Donna Gaines and realized her brilliantly colored hair belied the network of deeply etched wrinkles on her face. She had to be in her eighties or older.

While she was looking at the other participants, Margaret fell behind in balancing on the chair for back kicks. A bit embarrassed, she fell into the rhythm, although the gentle exercise seemed too easy to be of much benefit.

"It's awfully warm in here today," Donna said beside her. "They must have the thermostat set at ninety."

Her face was moist, and her glowing hair was wilting on her forehead. Margaret hadn't noticed the temperature one way or the other, but she was surprised to realize the Gaines woman was making hard work of the simple exercises.

Maybe she was missing something, but Margaret found the SeniorClass routine too easy to have much aerobic benefit for her. The reason was no mystery. She was easily the youngest person in the room except for the instructor.

"Nice seeing you here, Margaret," Augie said on the way out after forty-five minutes of slow-motion exercising. "Nothing like a workout to get the blood pumping and the brain cells producing."

"Nothing like it," Margaret agreed, although not in the way he meant. She felt as though she'd wasted an hour when she could've been painting. Moving her brush over the canvas would have burned more calories.

Putting on her coat and listening to Donna's chitchat, Margaret felt like a modern Goldilocks. One class was too hard; the other was too easy. She couldn't keep in step with the young people, but the SeniorClass only exercised her jaw. She couldn't seem to stop yawning. Much as she admired the elderly members of the class for keeping in shape in their eighties and older, she wasn't ready for geriatric workouts.

At least she'd walked to the community center, which gave her a little real exercise. She felt too restless to go home and work on her lighthouse in winter painting. It still wasn't going very well. No doubt she'd work it out, but she didn't feel inspired after the lackluster workout.

Her wristwatch showed it was after one o'clock, and she wondered whether Allan had picked up Adelaide. She generally only worked half a day on Monday because Shelley's busiest time came later in the week when people put in orders for the weekend. On impulse, Margaret decided to stop at her friend's house.

Shelley came to the door wearing a white chef's jacket, rather a surprise because she usually worked in her everyday clothes. Her cheeks were pink from the heat of her kitchen, and Margaret worried she was intruding on her baking.

"Allan left a few minutes ago with Adelaide," Shelley said, "but please come in."

"I don't want to bother you if you're busy baking."

"You won't be. Tami is using the oven for a new black walnut cookie recipe. I'm not sure the people at the Cove will like them, but there's no stopping her when she gets an idea." Shelley sounded so discouraged Margaret was concerned.

"Where did you get the black walnuts? They're difficult to get out of their shells. I like the taste in baked goods, but what a lot of work they are."

"Tami talked me into buying a big bag of pieces at the market. They were expensive though." She took Margaret's coat and led the way to the kitchen, now the heart of her home.

"Where are the kids?"

"Dan took them to the Mercantile. It's the one store in town where the kids can do a lot of looking and not much spending. Aiden has a little money from his grandparents burning a hole in his pocket."

"I imagine it's a fun place for kids to shop, such long aisles and so much variety," Margaret said.

"Yes, although I debated whether to let Aiden go. He had another of his mysterious tummyaches last night. He seemed okay this morning, but I wonder whether I should take him to the doctor."

"Sometimes it's a hard decision," Margaret sympathized, "especially when there are no lasting symptoms."

They walked into the kitchen where Shelley's helper was taking a pan of cookies from the oven. She was wearing the same type of heavily starched white chef's jacket as Shelley.

"You both look so professional in those coats," Margaret said after greeting Tami.

"They were Tami's idea. We get them from a laundry service that does most of the restaurants in the area."

Shelley didn't sound happy about the extra expense, and Margaret wondered why she'd gone along with it.

"We're only using the service on a trial basis," Shelley added. "They furnish dish towels too. I have to admit it saves on laundry, and I'm always behind on mine."

"You're just in time to try one of my black walnut cookies," Tami said, carefully transferring them from the baking sheet to a cooling rack. "Just give them a few minutes to cool."

"Not for me, thanks," Margaret said, although the aroma of freshly baked cookies tested her willpower. "I just came from an exercise class. One cookie would undo what little benefit I got from it."

"What class was that?" Shelley asked, putting on the teakettle.

"SeniorClass, but I won't be going again. The average age of the participants was mideighties or older."

"While you two ladies are visiting, maybe I should run over to the community center to get your plates before something happens to them," Tami said.

"I'm sure they're safe, but that would be nice of you," Shelley said, draping tea bags in two mugs.

Margaret was quiet while Shelley made tea for the two of them. She sensed her friend wanted to talk, but not until her helper had left.

"She seems to make herself useful," Margaret said after Tami was gone.

"Überuseful. In fact, some mornings I feel like staying in bed and letting her run my business. She knows so much more about baking than I do."

"I'm sure that's not true," Margaret said sympathetically. "There's a lot more to a successful business than just producing the product. I've found that out from my gallery."

"Look around," Shelley said unhappily. "She's reorganized my kitchen, and I have to admit it's more efficient. We have lists for shopping and a signup sheet to use the oven. Now she has me wearing professionally laundered jackets and using towels delivered every week by a service. My whole operation has been upgraded, and I'm worried about the bottom line."

"You're getting a wonderful reputation. The people at the Garden Club fund-raiser raved about your refreshments. They'd never tasted anything as unique as the little crème horns."

"They were Tami's."

"Well, they loved everything. Though I'm ashamed to say I had two of your lemon bars. They were so luscious I couldn't resist—much as I should have."

"Thanks, Margaret. I needed to hear that. I'm just worried my baking isn't as good as Tami's. Maybe my customers will be disappointed when they only have my stuff. I mean, she's trained in the culinary arts. She has an apprenticeship in an upscale New York restaurant waiting for her after she graduates," Shelley said. "Tami will go back to the school at the end of the month. I suppose I can return to doing everything the way I used to, but should I? She knows so much about baking. Maybe I'm in over my head."

Margaret paused. "Would you like to know what my advice would be?"

Shelley nodded.

"Take what you can learn from her but stay true to yourself. You know what people in Marble Cove like, and you do it sensationally well. Have you ever had a complaint?"

"No, I guess not."

"There! You see? The business is built on your delicious cookies, not on fancy items no one here has ever tried before."

"Thanks, Margaret. You're certainly good for my morale. And I haven't even asked how you're doing. Are you painting much?" Shelley asked.

"Every chance I get. Besides getting ready for the summer season at the gallery, I'm busy creating pieces that Matt Beauregard is going to use on merchandise other than greeting cards."

"You mean like calendars and mugs? I often buy that kind of thing at the Hermit Crab for gifts," Shelley told her eagerly. "The owner of the gift shop said they're items that sell well, and that was last fall after the tourist season was over."

"I'm really eager for warm weather," Margaret mused. "But I wonder if Beverly will be here to share it with us."

"Why? Did she get the job in Chicago?"

"I don't know, but I will miss her if she leaves," Margaret said.

"She certainly makes life more interesting. If anyone can find buried treasure in Marble Cove, I'm thinking it would be Beverly. She thinks outside the box."

"If there is a treasure," Margaret said. "Not to be pessimistic, but Jeremiah Thorpe could've been writing about heavenly rewards."

Margaret glanced at her watch and knew she should be going, but it was fun to talk about possible treasure.

"We'll really need Beverly if we're ever going to solve the mystery of the lost treasure, don't we?" Shelley asked. "She's a member of Old First and may be able to find someone who can shed some light on the church's history."

"Right now we don't have a starting place. Even if Beverly leaves, I'd love to keep working on the mystery."

"I hope she gets the job if that's what she wants," Shelley said, "but I really would miss her for more reasons than treasure hunting."

"I do hope she'll do what's best for her," Margaret said, "but it's always hard to have a friend move away. I'd better get going now. Allan will be waiting to hear how I liked the SeniorClass."

"Thanks for coming by. Can I make up a plate of cookies for your family?"

"I'd love to say yes, but all three of us need to cut down on sweets."

"I won't tempt you then," Shelley said with a light laugh. "And thanks for trying to boost my confidence. Tami is a blessing, I know she is, but sometimes I don't feel up to her standards."

"There's no reason for you to feel that way," Margaret assured her as she went to collect her coat. "Remember:

your business is booming because you know what the folks in Marble Cove like."

She hurried home, eager to get out of the biting wind. The SeniorClass was largely forgotten, but Margaret was troubled by a persistent feeling of sadness. Would Beverly be there to help them find Jeremiah Thorpe's lost treasure?

CHAPTER FIFTEEN

Diane was working on the germ of an idea Monday afternoon, and the last thing she wanted was to be interrupted for no reason—again. But this time it might be someone who actually had information about Rocky, so she reluctantly reached for the cell phone sitting beside her computer.

"Are you the one who put up fliers about a missing dog?" a rather gruff female voice asked.

"Yes, he's a yellow Lab/golden retriever mix and answers to the name Rocky. Have you seen a dog like that?"

"Nope, but my German shepherd just had five of the cutest little pups you ever saw. I don't have papers for them, so I can let you have pick of the litter for an even two hundred."

"I'm really not interested in a new dog," Diane said as patiently as she could. "I want to find the one I had."

"Oh, he's probably in the next county by now," the woman said. "You'd do better to come look at my puppies. If the price is too high, we can haggle a little."

"No, really, I'm not in the market for a puppy."

"You're making a mistake. No breed is easier to train than a German shepherd."

"Thank you for calling," Diane said, abruptly ending the conversation.

She was beginning to regret putting up the posters, but she missed Rocky terribly. Her notices had brought results, but not the one she'd hoped for. So far three people had spotted dogs running loose and called her, but one turned out to be a Shetland sheepdog belonging to a local farmer. Another was a mutt whose coat was vaguely similar to Rocky's, and the third sounded more like a pit bull than her pet. Nor had Leo Spangler come up with any leads through his veterinary practice. He had been checking in with her regularly to offer his support and she was touched by his concern for her. Maybe she should give him another chance to win her heart.

As if the false sightings weren't bad enough, she'd been solicited to donate to a society for runaway dogs. The person had quickly hung up when Diane said she was checking out their charity rating on her computer as they spoke. It made her angry that a con artist would take advantage of a dog owner searching for a lost pet, but that was one battle she couldn't fight.

Her most poignant call was from a child of perhaps eight or ten. His parents were going to get rid of a puppy that had proved difficult to handle, and the boy wanted to find a good home for him. An adult made him hang up before she could learn more.

"Rocky, where are you?" she asked, looking at the spot where he liked to nap while she worked.

She'd left his big rawhide bone beside her desk in hopes he'd soon return and claim it. In fact, there were reminders of Rocky throughout the house. Until he'd gone missing, she hadn't realized how many of his things were scattered throughout her cottage. She'd scrubbed out his water and food dishes and laundered the cover of his dog bed. His toys were in a net bag, and the brush she used to groom him was still under the kitchen sink. His collar and license were hanging on the peg board she'd installed for his leash, a sad reminder he'd gotten loose without them. She just couldn't forgive herself for being so absentminded she didn't fully close the back door.

Returning to her computer, she couldn't summon up the idea she'd had for the next scene. She tried to think positive thoughts, and certainly the release of her first book next month was cause for joy.

This evening she'd invited Margaret, and Shelley to come by for an impromptu party for Beverly, whose birthday was the next day. Possibly it would also be an impromptu good-bye party for Beverly, although that prospect did nothing to lift her spirits. She wished there were some good advice she could give her friend, but anything she might say would be tinged with regret at the possibility of losing her.

"It's not about you," she told herself.

The important thing was that any decision Beverly made should be beneficial for her. Maybe Marble Cove was too small for a smart, talented person like Beverly to realize her full potential.

Diane felt greatly blessed to be able to work from her home, although lately she'd been letting herself down by not accomplishing what she should on her second book. Somewhere she'd lost the drive and creativity to produce a worthy sequel to her first successful sale. Missing Rocky and worrying about Beverly were only the latest excuses not to be moving forward on her next mystery novel. She very much wanted to get back on track, but so far she wasn't very successful.

Instead of writing, she turned again to Jeremiah Thorpe's letters. They fascinated her, and almost every day she managed to decipher another word or phrase. But one they'd managed to make out last month kept returning to her mind: "a fortuitous maritime Discovery." But what exactly did that mean? Could it mean something besides treasure, as they'd all assumed?

Apparently Thorpe had retrieved something from a shipwreck and hidden it away. He'd left clues in his letter, perhaps wanting it to be an inheritance for his family or a legacy for the future of the settlement.

Diane fervently wished her fictional mystery stimulated her imagination as much as Thorpe's letters. Maybe this evening her friends would have some ideas about what to do next in the treasure hunt.

★   ★   ★

Shelley was pleased to be going to Diane's. Since she stopped working out of the Cove, she rarely left Dan to take care of the children in the evening, but he'd been cheerful about it.

"You've been working hard," he told her when she expressed doubt about going. "The kids and I will have fun. After Emma goes to bed, Aiden and are I going to have a hoops contest."

Their latest game was to throw a foam rubber ball into a small hoop attached to his bedroom door. Her son loved trying to score points against his dad, and he practiced with Adelaide to improve his aim.

"Don't forget to powder Emma really well before you put her down for the night. She gets rashes so easily."

"Honey, I'm on top of it. Go have a good time with your friends."

"Thanks, Dan. I won't be late."

"I'll leave the porch light on so you can see to walk home. Be careful. We're supposed to get freezing rain or sleet later tonight."

"I'm only going next door," Shelley said, giving Emma a bedtime kiss and hugging Aiden.

He tried to wiggle free, but he still wanted all the details on where she was going and when she would be home.

"Go to sleep nicely for Daddy," she said, pulling on her winter jacket, hoping he wouldn't have a tummyache while she was gone.

On the short walk to Diane's, she wished she hadn't left home without her woolen scarf. Winter seemed to be lasting forever this year, or maybe she was just eager for nice sunny days when the kids could play outdoors. She couldn't help but wish warmer weather might bring better job prospects for Dan. He was trying hard to be supportive and helpful at home, but she knew it bothered him that it was her business that was keeping them afloat.

She was the first to arrive, and Diane greeted her as she took the red velvet cake out of her hands.

"Come in by the fire," she said.

Before Shelley could seat herself on Diane's comfy couch, the bell rang. Margaret and Beverly came in together, and Shelley felt warm and happy being with the three of them.

"Happy birthday!" they chorused as they gave Beverly a group hug.

"We wanted to surprise you and celebrate just a little early," Diane said.

"This is very sweet of you all," Beverly told them as Diane took her coat. "I've been so busy considering what to do about this job, I guess I all but forgot about my birthday."

"Naturally we have a fabulous Lighthouse Sweet Shoppe cake," Diane said with a grin. "I thought we'd have it here in the living room with a pot of green tea."

"Sounds wonderful to me," Margaret said, shedding her coat and handing it to Diane to hang up. "I don't understand why March seems colder than January."

"Maybe because we're all so tired of the cold," Beverly said. "We expect to shiver a lot in midwinter, but enough is enough."

They talked around the subject on all their minds for several minutes while Diane brought out the teapot and slices of Shelley's delicious red velvet cake. She served it on her best bone china plates with gold rims.

Shelley was dying to know whether Beverly was leaving, but like the others, she skirted around the big question.

"Delicious cake," Margaret said. "As usual."

"I know what you're waiting to hear," Beverly said after she took a small bite of cake. "I did get an offer for the job in Chicago. I initially turned it down, but they sweetened the pot with a guarantee of six weeks of vacation every year so I can make frequent visits to see my father."

"Does that mean you accepted their second offer?" Shelley asked.

"No, not yet. It's the hardest decision I've ever had to make. It's a once-in-a-lifetime chance, but I hate leaving Marble Cove and especially all of you. You can be sure I've been losing sleep over it since I first got invited for an interview."

"Would your father move with you?" Margaret asked.

"I wish! Maybe he'll change his mind later, especially if his health problems get worse, but he's pretty insistent on staying here for now. Still, it would be really hard to leave him."

"How does he feel about the offer?" Diane asked.

"Fortunately, he's very supportive of the change if it's what I want. In fact, he urged me to take the job, but I'm worried about him. I know he has help from Mrs. Peabody, and the community looks after its own. But I'm the only family he has. I don't know whether the job is worth the worry, being so far from him."

"I'd miss you terribly," Diane said, "but I would be happy for your sake."

"It sounds like a wonderful opportunity," Margaret agreed, "but you're very close to your father. I wouldn't want to choose between family and a great job."

"I can see how hard the decision must be for you," Shelley said.

In some ways Beverly was her role model, a smart, self-confident woman who'd rallied from her husband's death. Beverly's advice had been invaluable as she launched her baking business.

"If you decide to take the job, when would you have to leave?" Diane asked.

"They'd like me to be there in Chicago by the first of April, but I'm trying to negotiate for more time. After all, I have to give the State House proper notice and it's a big move halfway across the country. The prospect of relocating so far from here is pretty daunting. One minute I decide to take the plunge, and the next I feel anxious about leaving my father. I've never agonized this much over any decision."

Shelley allowed herself a moment of hope. Beverly didn't sound convinced she should take the new job, but when she went on to describe it, she obviously was very excited by the prospect of working for a large company.

"If the people I would work with are as nice as the head of human relations, it should be a pleasant place to work. Of course, there's no way I can know that until I actually begin work there. I suspect there's a lot of competition for advancement."

"If you decide to take the job, we'll all be delighted for your sake. And remember, you'll only be seconds away by phone or Internet," Margaret said.

"But how are we going to solve the mystery of the missing treasure without our number-one sleuth?" Shelley asked.

"Me? You flatter me," Beverly said with a laugh. "I'm curious, but that doesn't make me much of a detective. Diane is a much better detective than I am."

Diane laughed. "That's one of the reasons I wanted all of us to get together tonight. Instead of working on my book, I've been obsessed with reading and rereading Jeremiah Thorpe's letters. As scratchy and faded as his writing is, I continue to decipher bits and pieces. I made copies of what we have so far for all of you."

She reached over to an end table and picked up a pile of papers. "The blanks are words I haven't been able to make out."

"Seeing it this way is great," Shelley said as she read. "It's beginning to make sense."

"He wanted someone to know his secret about a hidden treasure. That much is clear," Margaret said.

"I suspect he may have been ill when he wrote it," Diane said. "Just before he passed away, my grandfather's handwriting got squiggly like Thorpe's."

"What do we have to go on?" Beverly asked. "If he did hide something of value, do we have any clue to its whereabouts?"

"Look at page three of my translation," Diane said. "I made out the words 'earthen hollow.' That seems to suggest he buried something."

"Or someone," Margaret said with a shudder. "There was a high death rate among the early settlers."

"If you were a minister, where would you bury something to keep it safe?" Shelley asked.

"I see where you're going," Beverly said. "He probably wanted to keep it close and easy to find."

"But not in a place where someone could accidentally find it. That must be why the letters were in the old tower, but the treasure wasn't," Margaret said.

A sudden picture came into Shelley's head, and she blurted out, "The graveyard."

"Of course," Beverly said. "It would be the best possible place. He could bury it in the cemetery. One of the graves would serve as a marker to find it again."

"No one would disturb the dead by digging around a burial spot. He could count on it not being discovered by accident," Diane said.

"Also a cemetery is creepy. You wouldn't find people digging for fishing worms or anything else in a place like that," Shelley said with a shudder.

"Let's assume he did use the cemetery," Beverly said. "He would've chosen the gravestone of someone who died before he did, so that eliminates later ones."

"And he would choose an area that wasn't likely to be disturbed by new burials," Diane said. "That probably means the oldest section of the original cemetery."

"The graveyard seems probable," Margaret said. "Too bad we don't have X-ray vision to see underground."

"Maybe we do!" Shelley was so excited she stood up. "What was the trunk like, the one where you found the letters?"

"It was basically a wooden box with iron bands and a crude lock. The key was still in the keyhole, or we wouldn't have been able to open it," Beverly said.

"So if the treasure is in a similar box, parts of it must be metal," Shelley said.

"I think I see where you're going," Margaret said excitedly. "Allan and I used to go beachcombing with a metal detector. We actually found a few coins and other odd bits. We even found a class ring and turned it in to the police, but no one ever claimed it. I think we still have the metal detector somewhere."

"Dan and his friends were into metal detectors when they were in their teens. They found quite a few coins—even a few old silver ones—on the school playground until the principal kicked them off. He objected to them digging up plugs of grass to find things. Dan was disappointed because he dug up more junk than treasure. I think his old metal detector is still stored in the eaves of the garage."

"I think we're onto something here," Beverly said. "It wouldn't be too intrusive to walk through the oldest part of the cemetery with metal detectors."

"I'm a little leery of Reverend Locke," Diane said. "He doesn't seem to have the slightest bit of curiosity about Jeremiah Thorpe or church history."

"No, but it would make his congregation very happy if we found something of value to pay for badly needed repairs and renovations on Old First," Beverly said.

"I suppose we could search the cemetery at night when no one is likely to be around," Margaret said. "It's not as if we would be digging or destroying anything."

"It sounds awfully scary to me," Shelley said.

"And cold!" Margaret said emphatically.

"What we need is a nice dark night when it isn't so cold we'll get frostbite," Diane said. "And we certainly want to include you, Beverly, so it has to be this month in case you decide to move to Chicago."

"I'd hate to leave Marble Cove without at least trying to find Thorpe's treasure," Beverly said. "Why don't we watch the weather? If it warms up a bit, we'll have a go at it. Are you all willing?"

"If the metal detectors are still working," Margaret said.

"I'm sure Dan would be happy to check them out. In fact, he'd probably like to do a little beachcombing before the summer people get here. He seems to have forgotten all about his old metal detector."

"That would be great if he could get his and Allan's working," Margaret said. "The four of us can cover the whole cemetery area if we use two detectors."

"We'll do it!" Beverly said decisively. "As soon as we get a break in the cold, we'll do it."

"A night without snow would be nice. We don't want to leave footprints in the cemetery. Imagine what a stir that would cause," Margaret said.

"It would be nice if it isn't raining too," Shelley said. "Muddy footprints in the churchyard cemetery would really irritate Reverend Locke if he's as cross as he seems."

"He's really a very good man," Beverly said in his defense. "He simply has a different point of view. I think he just wants us to be respectful of the church and of the past. But to be perfectly honest, it's going to be terribly hard to raise enough money to do all that needs to be done at Old First. Bake sales and silent auctions aren't going to do it, and members of the congregation aren't wealthy enough to fund it all by donations. I'm sure Reverend Locke would change his attitude if we find Thorpe's treasure."

"I should be getting home now," Shelley said, "but I'll have Dan look for his metal detector tomorrow and see if he can get it running."

"I'll drop ours off at your house so Dan can take a look at it."

"I'll watch the weather and find a time when we can all go," Beverly said.

"Meanwhile, I'll keep working on the letters," Diane promised. "I have a feeling there are still clues to be found."

After the group finished visiting, Shelley walked the short distance to her house with her head full of speculation about Thorpe's treasure. She had to caution Dan not to say anything to anyone before they searched the graveyard. Part of her could hardly wait to begin their search, but she was scared too. She wasn't very comfortable out after dark, and a cemetery was the last place she wanted to be in the dead of night.

As she walked home, she couldn't help but wonder. Were they kidding themselves about hidden treasure, or was there really something really precious out there waiting to be discovered?

CHAPTER SIXTEEN

I'm not sure, but I think I saw a golden retriever on the elementary school playground," Tami said, taking off her coat at Shelley's house Tuesday morning. "Could it be your friend's missing dog?"

"You didn't see any sign of an owner?"

"No, but I was driving. There were cars dropping children off in front of the school, so I couldn't pay much attention to the dog."

"If you're sure about the dog's color, it's worth letting Diane know," Shelley said. "I'll give her a call."

Diane sounded sad when she answered her phone, but she quickly perked up.

"It's the most promising lead I've had so far this week," she said. "I'll circle around the area in my car right away in case it really was Rocky."

"Let me know whether you find him," Shelley said. "Tami and I will be waiting to hear from you."

"I hope I didn't give her false hope," Tami said. "I don't know much about dog breeds, but it definitely had a gold-colored coat."

"Diane is more than happy to follow any lead. She's been frantic with worry."

"I don't blame her. Whenever I see an animal beside the road, I slow down. It would be so easy to hit one."

"I guess we should get to work," Shelley said. "There's a bridge tournament at the community center tomorrow. The person in charge wants cookies the players can eat and still play at the same time. Nothing sticky or crumbly. I was thinking of almond crisps for one item. Do you have any ideas?"

The doorbell rang before Tami could answer.

"Adelaide is here," Shelley said, scooping Emma out of her playpen and hurrying to the front foyer.

"Good morning," she said warmly, welcoming her helper as she put her daughter down to toddle up to Adelaide. "I'm so glad to see you! Aiden is in his room hoping to shoot hoops with you. The kids have had breakfast, but Emma is still in her pajamas, as you can see. I laid out the outfit with cherries on the shirt, but I didn't have time to dress her."

She left Adelaide to hang up her coat and chase down Emma. Not surprisingly, Tami already had bowls and measuring cups on the counter and was assembling ingredients.

"I found some anise extract in your spice cupboard. I thought it could be used to flavor Springerle since you have the custom rolling pin to create them."

"Oh dear, I'd almost forgotten I have it."

"I noticed the original wrapper is still on it."

"Yes, it was a gift from my mother-in-law a few years ago. I've never used it," Shelley said.

"It will be so much fun to roll out the dough with fancy designs, and the cookies will be hard and rather dry, not at all messy for bridge players."

"I'm not sure about anise. Some people don't like the licorice flavor," Shelley said, although she liked the idea of decorative cookies. "All the recipes I've seen using anise suggest storing them in airtight containers for a couple of weeks to get the best flavor."

"I'd forgotten about that," Tami admitted. "Guess I still have a few things to learn."

"It's still a good idea," Shelley said. "We can flavor them with lemon zest. Would you like to make them?"

"I'd love to if you're sure you don't want to roll them out yourself."

"No, it was your idea."

It was such a good idea Shelley wished she had thought of it herself. Why did Tami always come up with such clever ideas? She'd pretty much forgotten about the rolling pin with carved designs made especially for Springerle. They would be perfect for nibbling during a bridge tournament.

Adelaide had to leave at lunchtime for a dentist appointment, but by then Shelley had finished an order for whoopie pies, two soft chocolate cookies with a luscious white filling sandwiched between them. They went into the freezer until Saturday. A birthday boy didn't like cake, so his mother and Shelley had hit upon the whoopie pies. They were her son's favorite treat and thick enough to hold candles.

"If there's nothing else to be done right now, I'm going to get my hair cut," Tami said.

"No, Tuesday is a slow day. There's nothing urgent for this afternoon. I'll use cookies from the freezer for the Cove."

"Bye, then." She walked through to the dining area and stopped.

"Hey, Aiden, what's the trouble?" Tami asked.

"I want Mama."

"I'm right here," Shelley said. "What's wrong?"

"I don't feel good."

"Where don't you feel good?"

"My tummy."

"Wow, I hope you don't have Mr. Flu," Tami said sympathetically. She turned to Shelley. "If you need me to stay..."

"No, but thanks for offering," Shelley said.

Maybe Tami could outbake her in the kitchen, but she still knew more about mothering.

She took Aiden's temperature, and it was normal. His stomach didn't seem to hurt in one specific place, and he had her baffled. Was she overlooking the obvious?

One thing was certain: her son really didn't feel well. He lay down on his bed and whimpered, refusing her offer of apple juice, his favorite drink.

Emma was playing quietly in her room, although ordinarily she would be curious about what Aiden was doing. Shelley tried to comfort him, then went to check on her daughter.

Emma was sitting in the middle of the floor, surrounded by toys but ignoring them. She had a little paper sack in one hand and what appeared to be a pink candy. Her face was smeared, and she was grinning like a little monkey. Prize sat beside her, watching expectantly for a doggy treat. Fortunately, Emma didn't seem to have shared. At least she wouldn't have a sick dog on her hands.

"Emma, where did you get that?"

Shelley knew the answer, of course, as she gently took it away. Only one business in town sold candy in bulk, the kind that tasted like candy corn but came in different colors, and dispensed it in brown paper bags: the Mercantile.

"What on earth are you doing with this?" she asked her daughter, not expecting an answer.

She scooped Emma up and realized she was sticky from her hairline to her socks. Apparently she'd chewed it with her new teeth and let it dribble out of her mouth. Shelley washed her face and hands, then gingerly stripped off her daughter's soiled clothes and popped her back into her pajamas. She would have to wait until the laundry was done for a new outfit. It might be a job to get the stains out, but more importantly, what did Aiden know about this?

Walking into Aiden's room with Emma in tow, she asked, "Where did your sister get this candy?"

"Adelaide brought us a treat. She bought it with her very own money."

"How many pieces did you eat?"

Aiden sat up looking miserable, and held out all the fingers on both hands.

"You ate ten pieces of candy without asking me?"

He didn't need to answer. Judging by how empty the bag was, he'd eaten enough to give him another stomachache.

"That's why your tummy has been hurting. How did Emma get the bag?"

"She took it off my shelf. She's always getting into my stuff," he whined. "I don't feel good."

"No wonder," Shelley said, disappointed in Adelaide and more than a little irritated with her son. He knew he wasn't supposed to eat sweets without asking her. "I'll get you a little tablet you can chew for your tummy, but I hope you've learned not to eat candy without my permission."

Adelaide had never before given the children candy or anything else to eat without checking with her. Shelley hated to call Margaret, but she couldn't let this pass. She adored Adelaide and greatly appreciated her patience and kindness, but sharing a bag of candy with the kids was an absolute no-no.

She placed the call reluctantly, almost hoping Margaret wouldn't answer. She did.

"I have a little problem," Shelley began, trying to decide the most tactful way to approach Margaret. "Aiden has been having tummyaches, and this morning I found Emma with one of the candy bags from the Mercantile."

"Oh my! You're calling me. That means Adelaide must have given it to them."

"I'm afraid so. I confiscated a bag with the kind they sell in bulk. And I don't think it's the first time it's happened."

"Oh dear." Margaret sounded distressed.

Shelley was sorry to upset her friend, but she couldn't let it happen again. Emma may have dribbled out more than she ate, but Aiden definitely overdid it.

"I know what happened," Margaret said. "Allan has been letting Adelaide shop alone in the Mercantile while he does other errands. She's been excited to spend some of her babysitting money."

She paused. "Oh dear. I suspect Adelaide has bought candy every time she and Allan have gone. We were proud of her for buying a little bottle of nail polish for me and a package of chewing gum for her dad. She must have bought the candy as a surprise for Aiden. I'm sure she meant to be kind to him, although it isn't like her to give it to Emma. She understands about babies choking."

"According to Aiden, his sister snitched it from his room," Shelley said. "I hated to call, but obviously it can't happen again."

"No, of course not," Margaret quickly agreed. "Allan took her to the dentist, but we'll have a talk as soon as they get home. I hope you still trust her to sit with your children."

"Of course," Shelley said emphatically. "I don't know what I'd do without her. I'm sure she only wanted to do something nice. Truthfully, Aiden is to blame too. He knows better than to stuff candy in his mouth without asking me."

"He's only a little boy," Margaret said. "Allan and I will see it doesn't happen again. We'll talk with Adelaide. Thank you for telling me."

"I'm so grateful for Adelaide's help. I don't want her to be scolded." Shelley felt bad about the call, even though she had to protect her children from unwise gifts.

"We want her to be able to do more things on her own, but I guess we still need to give her a little more guidance on her shopping choices."

★   ★   ★

Margaret was disappointed but not angry with her daughter. It was so like Adelaide to give a small treat to her little friend. Unfortunately, the candy hadn't been an appropriate gift.

Allan and Adelaide came home with happy faces.

"That wasn't as bad as I thought it'd be," her daughter happily reported.

"Yes, she was very calm when they did the filling. She just needs to keep brushing and flossing." Allan added. "She won't need to go back for awhile."

"I'm glad to hear that," Margaret said. She was relieved everything went smoothly but she didn't want to put off the talk about the candy.

"We'd better sit at the table for a team meeting," she said. Whenever they had something important to discuss, that's what they called it.

"What's up?" Allan asked, hanging his plaid wool jacket over the back of a chair and sitting down.

Adelaide took her usual place at the table and looked at her mother expectantly.

"Adelaide, it was very nice of you to buy gifts for us and Aiden with the money you earned," Margaret began, "but we have a small problem."

Adelaide's expression changed from happy to puzzled.

"Candy really isn't good for young children," Margaret went on. "Aiden has been getting tummyaches from eating too much. Today Emma got hold of the sack and helped herself. I know you meant well, Adelaide, but next time show Shelley what you're giving the children."

"I didn't know she'd been buying candy," Allan said with a guilty expression. "I should've stayed with her while she shopped."

"No, we agreed to let her try shopping on her own. I'm not angry, dear," she quickly said, seeing Adelaide on the verge of tears. "It was generous and kind of you to think of others, only promise me you won't give Aiden or Emma anything else to eat."

"I promise, Mom," Adelaide solemnly promised. "No more candy."

"And if you buy them a little present in the future, will you show it to me or Shelley first?"

Adelaide nodded.

"Now why don't you find Oreo? Your kitty hasn't played with his ball of yarn in a long time," Margaret suggested.

When Adelaide left the kitchen, Allan turned to Margaret with a worried expression.

"I guess we shouldn't let her shop on her own anymore. I should've paid more attention to what she bought."

"It's my fault too," Margaret said. "We didn't give her any guidelines on what she could or couldn't buy. I'm proud she thought of others, not herself, when she spent her babysitting money."

"You're right," Allan said, his shoulders slumping. "Next time I'll ask her to show me what she bought. Or maybe I could stand at the front of the store and watch her check out. That way, she can still feel independent, but I'll know what she buys."

"Either way would be okay," Margaret agreed. "I can't help but worry, though. What will our daughter do when we're not here to take care of her?"

"We're laying the groundwork for that now and she will be okay when the time comes," he said, walking over to take Margaret in his arms. "Meanwhile, our plan is still good. We'll teach her to do as many things as possible. Handling money and shopping on her own are important skills. She understands the concept. She just needs a little more practice."

Margaret nodded, then stood. "I think I'll take a walk even if it is cold," she said. "It will give me a chance to clear my head. Do you want to come with me?"

"Love to, but I have to put another coat of varnish on the hutch I'm making. I promised to deliver it by next week."

Margaret bundled up in her warmest winter wear, wrapping her navy and green striped scarf around her neck. In the coldest weather, she liked to breathe into it to stay warm, but fortunately, the temperature was slowly creeping up above freezing during the day.

Now it was the wind leeching the warmth from her body. People who'd never lived near a great body of water didn't realize how high humidity penetrated flesh and bone. Margaret wondered how long it would be before arthritis stiffened her joints and made walking more difficult. Maybe she didn't belong in an exercise class with octogenarians, but she wasn't getting any younger.

Walking was unpleasant, and she abandoned her idea of circling round the town. She'd only gone a block, so she cut over to the next street and decided to look in on Diane. She wouldn't stay if her friend was busy writing, but she did wonder whether there was any news about Rocky.

"Come in," Diane said with a broad smile. "You must have read my mind. I've been dying to talk to someone."

"I won't stay long. I know you must have writing to do."

"Actually, I got up early and made a little progress, but Shelley called. Her helper, Tami—have you met her?—saw a dog on the school playground and wondered if it could be Rocky. Naturally I hurried over."

Margaret looked around. "I don't see Rocky, so I guess it was a false alarm," she said, shedding her coat and handing it to Diane.

"Afraid so, but she did have the color of the coat right. Turns out the dog got out of a car when a mother was dropping off her children. I helped her catch him, so the trip wasn't a waste. Also she promised to watch for Rocky, so that's one more pair of eyes searching for him."

"We had a little drama of our own," Margaret said, telling her friend about Adelaide's gift of candy as she followed her to the kitchen and sat at the table.

Diane chuckled. "It was sweet of her, really. She thought of others instead of shopping for herself. You should be proud of her."

"I am, but I worry about her future. What will she do without Allan and me?"

"You're both in good health. You shouldn't have to worry any time soon."

"I pray we'll be with Adelaide for quite some time yet, but I'm not doing what I should to stay healthy. I'm too slow and out of sync to exercise with young people, but the SeniorClass wasn't much benefit."

"Is there something in between?" Diane asked, putting on the teakettle.

"Well, there is a tai chi class on the list at the community center, but I'm not even sure what that is exactly." She reached for a ginger snap from a plate Diane put on the table.

"Oh! I remember seeing groups doing tai chi in parks in Boston. It was like watching a slow, beautiful dance, with everyone moving in unison," Diane said. "I think you might like it. And the way it felt outside this morning, it will be quite a while before you can get back to swimming in the ocean."

"That's true."

Margaret laid the uneaten half of the ginger snap on a napkin. It wasn't enough to think or talk about changing her lifestyle. For her daughter's sake, she had to get serious about her health, and that meant more exercise. Much as she loved the time she spent painting and the short winter hours in her gallery, she needed to get herself moving.

She and Diane talked over steaming cups of herbal tea, but her mind wasn't on the Thorpe letters or the possibility Beverly might leave Marble Cove. She made up her mind to take a look at the exercise class with the obscure name. She had nothing to lose and everything to gain.

Even if tai chi did sound more like a restaurant entrée than an exercise.

Chapter Seventeen

"B reakfast is ready!" Mrs. Peabody's voice cut into Beverly's thoughts.

Beverly had told her several times it wasn't necessary to fix the morning meal for her. Although she greatly appreciated Mrs. Peabody's help in preparing her father's food, she wasn't used to eating on someone else's schedule. On nice warm days, she much preferred to do her morning run on the beach before breakfast.

"I need to check my e-mail and take care of a few business details before I eat," she said, coming into the kitchen to say good morning to her father.

"I made pancakes with whole wheat flour," the older woman said. "Better for your father than white flour."

Her father's helper was proud of adhering to a healthy menu, although she would never be convinced that Beverly's preference for seafood and poultry was a good thing.

"Maybe you can put mine in the oven to keep them warm for a little while," Beverly said to keep Mrs. Peabody happy, although she doubted she'd eat such a heavy breakfast.

Her father looked up from his stack of pancakes dripping sugar-free syrup, and it wasn't hard to read the question in his eyes: had she made a decision about the Chicago job?

She had. After another restless, dream-haunted night, she'd finally decided to accept the position. It was the opportunity of a lifetime, the kind she'd dreamed of. She needed a positive goal in her life, and the pharmaceutical company was offering personal advancement as well as a chance to contribute to the world's health.

"I'll talk to you in a little bit," she told her father.

He nodded and continued his attack on the crispy-edged pancakes.

He pushed away the turkey sausages Mrs. Peabody had cooked up. "These things are tasteless," Beverly heard him comment to Mrs. Peabody as she slipped away to her bedroom and opened her laptop. Her consulting business was really beginning to get off the ground, and she wondered whether she could keep up with it after she began the Chicago job. And would her new employer see her outside work as a conflict of interest? She hated to let her clients down after working so hard to secure them.

The first e-mail she read had nothing to do with business.

"Good morning, Beverly. Your favorite roving photographer is home from another adventure with some free time. How about a belated birthday dinner tonight? My mouth is watering for a seafood platter at Captain Calhoun's, but mostly I'm eager to see you. Is it a date? Hope to see you, Jeff."

Beverly very much wanted to talk to him about her opportunity in Chicago, so she quickly tapped out a reply, agreeing to have dinner with him.

Jeff came to her house ten minutes late and apologetic, but bearing a gorgeous bouquet of mixed roses.

"Sorry I'm late," he said coming inside to say hello to her father. "My grandfather was in a talkative mood, and that doesn't happen very often. He's drowning in seed catalogs and can't wait to start his garden. I guess he's a farmer at heart, even though he spent most of his career in the military."

"I know his neighbors and the people in assisted living homes really appreciate all the fresh produce he delivers to them," Beverly said.

"Well, you two kids have a nice dinner," her father said, dismissing them as he wandered back into his den again to immerse himself in his current book.

Beverly felt happier than she had in a long time. She'd spent an unusual amount of time getting ready, choosing to wear a long, silvery silk skirt with a teal blue top that was both blouse and shawl. She was probably overdressed to go out for dinner in Marble Cove, but she'd felt girlishly excited about her birthday date—or perhaps it was being with Jeff again.

True to his profession, Jeff rarely wore a suit, and tonight wasn't an exception. He was wearing a creamy white cable-knit sweater with new-looking jeans. On most men, the heavy weave would have made them look pudgy, but Jeff was slender and tall enough to wear it well. He hadn't bothered with a coat, although it was still frigid outside.

Getting her best black wool coat out of the closet, she handed it to Jeff, who was standing by to help her with it. Sometimes a woman enjoyed a little chivalry.

"Good night," she called out to her father. She didn't need to tell him not to wait up for her. He was rigid when it came to bedtime and would check out by ten o'clock.

"You look great tonight," Jeff said. "I should've brought my camera. I don't get to photograph a glamorous woman very often."

"You're exaggerating," she said with a pleased laugh. It felt good to be going out with a man she really liked.

By the time they drove the short distance to Captain Calhoun's a light snow was falling. Jeff's midnight black hair was sprinkled with fluffy flakes as they walked from the parking lot to the restaurant. The snow melted almost instantly as soon as they were inside, but dampness made the curl he usually cut away cling to the edge of his forehead.

"We have a reservation," he said to the hostess after hanging up Beverly's coat.

The place was surprisingly busy for a weeknight, but she remembered they offered Wednesday specials for senior citizens. When they were seated at a quiet corner table with a sparkling white tablecloth and a low-burning candle in a glass chimney, she had the illusion of being alone with Jeff.

Should she talk about her new job before dinner or after they'd eaten? She elected to eat first, knowing the meal would be spoiled if Jeff thought going to Chicago was a bad idea.

Jeff ordered Calhoun's famous seafood platter, but Beverly opted for lemon-garlic scallops served with wild rice and a crisp green salad. They traded bites of their entrées and laughed a lot, especially when Jeff related his latest adventures on the trail of unusual photographs.

"I'm never again going to lug my camera up the side of a volcano, no matter how much I get paid. But I did get some great angles. Hard to do in Hawaii where tourists are everywhere."

"You seem to enjoy your work a lot."

The waiter cleared the main course, and they both opted for coffee but not dessert.

"I wouldn't do it otherwise," he said, speaking more seriously than he had all evening. "Can you imagine me taking baby pictures or being cooped up in an office?" He laughed.

"No, I certainly can't." He'd given her the perfect opportunity to mention the new job. "I've been rethinking my career lately. Actually, I have a great offer, but it means moving to Chicago."

"What kind of job?"

"Financial officer at a pharmaceutical company. It's a wonderful opportunity and exactly the kind of work I'd like to be doing."

He sipped his coffee while she waited for some reaction from him.

"Sounds interesting," he said. "I didn't know you were job hunting."

"I wasn't. A headhunter approached me."

"How did your name come up?"

It was a good question, but she didn't have a very complete answer. "I'd sent my résumé to a headhunter several months ago and then forgotten all about it. Until I got a call to set up an interview. It basically came as a surprise."

He held up his hand and waved at their server, indicating he'd like more coffee. Beverly couldn't read his face, but he didn't seem affected one way or the other by her news.

"So, are you going to take it?" he asked after stirring sweetener into his coffee.

"I think I will, yes."

"It's a big decision," he mused, sipping his coffee. "When would you have to start work?"

"The first of next month."

"Is your father okay with it?"

"He's encouraged me to take it, but he refuses to move with me. I turned down their first offer, but they came back with more vacation time and a salary increase to make it easier to fly back to Maine and check on him."

"It sounds like a good opportunity," he said in a noncommittal voice.

"It is, but of course, it's a big step. I've never moved that far before. And Chicago can be an intimidating city, although I'll be working and living quite far north of the Loop."

"I have a friend who lives in Elgin but commutes into the city by train every day. If you need any advice about relocating, I can give you his e-mail address."

"Thanks, but someone in personnel will give me pointers. I'll only be renting at first."

"Good idea. Sometimes I think I'd be better off renting a couple of places instead of owning one. Of course, I'd like to have a base in Maine as long as my grandfather is alive."

Jeff asked a few more questions about what the job would entail, but he didn't comment in favor or against taking it. Beverly wasn't sure what she expected from him, but his whole reaction was nothing if not neutral.

After she'd told him all she could about the offer, she changed the subject, sharing with him the mystery of Jeremiah Thorpe's letters. He perked up and asked some really good questions.

"If you do find something of value, what will you do with it?" he asked.

"Give it to Old First to help with the renovations. The fund-raising dinner I organized last month didn't exactly yield stellar results, as you'll recall."

"Not many people would be that generous," he said with a warm smile.

They lingered at their table until it became clear the staff wanted them to leave so they could clean up and close. Somewhat to her surprise, since she'd only been paying attention to Jeff, all the other diners had left. They stepped out into a frigid wind, and she wondered aloud whether Chicago could possibly be as cold as Maine.

"Don't underestimate the lake effect," he said. "Lake Michigan is one whopping big body of water. I did a winter series about it for a travel magazine a few years ago. It was so cold I had to buy long johns just for the shoots."

On the short drive home, he talked about his latest assignment but didn't say anymore about her job offer.

Jeff put his arm around her shoulders as they walked up to her father's house from his car. A yellow glow from the front porch light illuminated their way, and she was sad to have the evening end.

"How long will you be in Marble Cove?" she asked before opening the door.

"I'm not sure. If something really good comes along, I'll take it. In my business, you never know from one week to the next. I wouldn't mind some time off, but turning down a choice assignment isn't smart. I'll keep in touch."

"Do that," she said, not surprised when he pulled her close and touched her lips with his.

He left without mentioning the Chicago job again. Beverly got ready for bed, not knowing whether to be hurt by his noncommittal attitude. He didn't seem to care if she took the job or not.

What did she expect him to say? Was she harboring a secret hope that he'd dissuade her from going because they would see even less of each other? Was he happy about her good prospects, or was it unimportant to him?

He traveled so much in his job, he probably had a different take on relocating. Certainly the distance from Maine to Illinois wasn't nearly as daunting to him as it was to her. Or maybe he didn't care where she worked.

They'd had a wonderful evening together, but was it just a way to pass the time for Jeff? Would he make the effort to see her if he didn't come to the area to see his grandfather?

The wonderful glow of being with him faded as she tried to puzzle out his mild reaction to her job offer.

When she was ready for bed, she remembered to put her cell phone on the charger. Somewhat to her surprise, there was a text message.

"Hi, Beverly. How about dinner with me Friday evening? I thought it might be fun to drive to Bangor. You can choose the restaurant. I'll call you tomorrow. Take care!"

Beverly wasn't entirely surprised by the message from Dennis Calder, but why was he asking her to go to Bangor with him? She liked Dennis well enough, but he could be a little full of himself and he hadn't been particularly supportive of her efforts at the Old First dinner and auction last month. She had hinted strongly that she wanted nothing more than friendship from him, but he didn't seem to be taking no for an answer.

She wondered how long Jeff would be in town. When would she see him again? He'd left her with a strong need to talk more about Chicago. Maybe he'd been too stunned to react. After all, she'd told him about it with no warning.

She reread the message from Dennis. There was just something about him she didn't really like, especially when she compared him to Jeff.

She sent him a text message politely refusing.

One thing was clear: her life was changing faster than she could absorb. She spent the last minutes before falling asleep wondering if she was doing the right thing by accepting the job. Was Jeff's lack of reaction a sign she was making a mistake? Would it doom any possible relationship with him? Would she regret leaving her father?

If the job was such a good idea, why did she still have reservations?

CHAPTER EIGHTEEN

Shelley picked up the phone in her kitchen, almost hoping it wasn't a customer—at least not one who wanted something special ready in a few hours. Thursday was often a busy day with people calling in orders for the weekend. As it was, she had to depend on Dan to make deliveries. He didn't mind doing them, but she tried not to give the impression he was working for her.

Emma was jumping up and down in her playpen wanting to get out, and Aiden had the TV on so loud she could hear it on the other side of the house. Both kids were still in their pajamas, and Dan had run over to his parents to borrow a book his father had on electrical work, a subject he was interested in learning about.

"Lighthouse Sweet Shoppe," she said, trying hard to sound chipper.

"Shelley, it's me," Margaret said. "I'm afraid Adelaide is coming down with a cold. I don't think she should be with your children today."

"Oh, I'll really miss her," Shelley said, "I hope she isn't feeling too sick."

"Her nose is stuffy, and she has a little cough," Margaret said. "I don't think she's sick enough to see a doctor, but she shouldn't be around Emma and Aiden. I'm sorry to let you down."

"It can't be helped. I hope she feels better soon."

Just as Shelley was hanging up, her daughter sent her sippy cup flying across the room. The plastic didn't break, but the lid came off, leaving a trail of orange juice to be mopped up.

"Naughty," Shelley scolded, although her rebuke didn't faze Emma, who was doing her best to climb out of the playpen by standing on her stuffed bear.

Shelley took the bear and sat her daughter down. "Now you have to stay there until I clean up your juice. It's all over the floor."

"Mama! I'm hungry," Aiden said, coming into the room.

"Watch where you're walking—you just walked right through Emma's spilled juice."

"I'm hungry!"

"You just had breakfast." She grabbed a paper towel and dried off the plastic on the foot of his pajamas.

"I didn't like that cereal."

He'd made his distaste plain at the breakfast table. Shelley had tried to save money by buying a large bag of generic cereal, but it was going to be a hard sell to get the family to eat all of it. She wondered if putting it in the brand-name box would help.

"You had toast too. You don't need anything until lunch."

"But, Mama! I need a cookie."

"No, you don't." Shelley knew better than to argue with her son. She was the boss, and everything didn't have to be a debate. "Now go turn off the TV."

"I want to watch my program."

"Every program is your program." She chided herself for making an issue of it. "Off now!"

Aiden shuffled out of the kitchen grumbling about how unfair she was.

She was down on her hands and knees, trying to clean up the mess without getting out her mop and pail. The juice was sticky, and she had to get a soapy rag to finish the job. In the process, she soaked one knee of her jeans and a strand of hair fell forward over her eyes.

"What happened here?" Tami asked, walking into the kitchen. "I rang the bell but no one answered."

"Emma managed to spill her juice. Aiden had the TV so loud I didn't hear you. But it doesn't matter. You're here now, and we have lots to do."

Tami looked calm, cool, and collected in a starched white chef's jacket. Her bright red hair was coiled on her head, and Shelley couldn't help but notice her fresh coat of coral nail polish. Her only bottle of polish was so old it had solidified from lack of use.

"There," Shelley said, standing upright. Her chef's jacket was wrinkled with stains of chocolate left from yesterday's baking, but she simply couldn't afford a fresh one for herself every day. When Tami left, the laundry service had to go. In fact, she was mad at herself for agreeing to the young woman's idea.

Tami was kneeling beside the playpen, cooing to Emma and capturing her attention.

"Would you like me to dress her before we start work?" she asked.

"Thanks, but she can wait until her father gets home. Adelaide has a cold and won't be coming over."

Shelley stood with the soapy rag dripping on her shoe, her children still in pajamas, and her husband off enjoying himself with his father. They probably went to the Cove for coffee and doughnuts, and she needed him now.

"What's first on the docket?" Tami asked in her usual cheerful voice. "Do you want me to frost the carrot cake?"

"Please. I put the cream cheese out to soften."

Her business was almost too good. Captain Calhoun's Crab and Lobster House wanted to add gourmet desserts to their menu, and they'd ordered the carrot cake and an array of tarts, including pecan spice and lemon custard.

Tami had used her own recipe for a dark carrot cake. It looked so luscious Shelley envied her success.

"I have to change out of my jeans," she said. "Are you all right for now?"

She scooped up Emma, knowing perfectly well Tami would get along fine without her. She seemed completely at home in the Bauer kitchen, so much so that Shelley sometimes felt in her way.

After changing Emma, she decided to dress her for the day and urged Aiden to dress himself. She went into her bedroom and stepped out of her damp jeans. As usual, she was way behind on laundry and had to settle for an old pair of black knit pants that should've gone to a charity shop years ago.

Aiden needed help with buttons, but finally all three of them were dressed. Now the problem was what to do with the kids until Dan could watch them. Of course, he couldn't take them along to make baked goods deliveries.

She gathered up an assortment of toys for Emma.

"Poor baby, you'll just have to stay in your pen until I figure out what to do. And Aiden," she called out, "you really do need to pick up your room. I think every toy you own is scattered around. When everything is in place, you can play."

She steeled herself to ignore his protests. There wasn't time for another mother-son debate.

Dan had been gone long enough. She called his parents' landline, and her mother-in-law answered.

"The men are off somewhere," Frances said.

"I badly need Dan to come home and help with the children," Shelley said, reluctantly confiding in his mother. "Adelaide is sick and can't watch them."

"Well, let me think. I was going to the market, but I could swing by afterward and pick them up."

"That would be nice of you. Dan needs to make some deliveries for me."

She was never comfortable imposing on Frances, but she didn't see an alternative. Even if she could afford a babysitter, all the young girls she knew were in school.

With Emma riding on her hip and a bag of toys in hand, she went back to the kitchen and deposited her unhappy daughter in the playpen. What did mothers do without them? They certainly didn't run home businesses.

Tami had finished frosting the carrot cake, and Shelley had to admit it was beautiful. Even the swirls of icing were artistic. She didn't think she'd ever have Tami's magic touch. She was skillful and sophisticated, setting the bar so high Shelley doubted she'd ever master all her helper's techniques.

Dear Lord, she silently prayed, *give me strength and patience. Sometimes I feel like I don't even know what I'm doing.*

"Who wants to lick the pan?" Tami asked, interrupting Shelley's prayer. "Is it all right if Aiden does? I'll put just a little on a spoon for Emma."

It wasn't all right, but Shelley didn't want to be a grouch with her children.

"Just a tiny taste for Emma. I'll get her plastic spoon. Aiden can lick, but try to scrape out most of it first. I've learned the hard way he doesn't do well with too much sugar."

"That's the nice thing about frosting a carrot cake with my cream cheese frosting. The cake is so sweet, I cut way back on the amount of confectioners' sugar in the icing. It's mostly cream cheese and butter."

Tami meant well, but Shelley was sure she should've said no to licking a bowl. She would regret it in the future if Aiden wanted to make a habit of it. Once again she'd let Tami lead her into a decision she really didn't want to make. Why did she let this sprite of a girl intimidate her?

She prayed to get beyond envy and resentment so she could appreciate all Tami was doing to help her. She might never be as sophisticated as Tami, but, with the Lord's guidance, she could accept Tami's superior skills with good grace.

★   ★   ★

Margaret was torn about leaving Adelaide. Her daughter was snuggled down under a colorful afghan on the couch. She'd put a small table beside her for a box of tissues and a cup of hot peppermint tea. Oreo was curled up by her feet, but Adelaide ignored her favorite cat. She definitely wasn't feeling well at all. Her nose was red and her eyes watery.

"Maybe I shouldn't go," Margaret said to her husband.

"Adelaide and I will be just fine," Allan assured her. "There's not much you can do about a cold. It just has to run its course."

"Yes, but..."

"Go try the new class. Maybe this tai chi is what you've been looking for."

"You can go, Mom," Adelaide croaked in a snuffly-sounding voice.

"All right," Margaret conceded, "but I'll be right home afterward."

She got ready and left the house, but it wasn't only concern for Adelaide that made her reluctant to try another class. Maybe group exercising just wasn't for her.

At the community center, she approached the exercise room with trepidation. Was this how Goldilocks felt when she was trying out the three bears' beds? She hoped her third try would be successful, but she wasn't optimistic.

Following the instructions she'd gotten when she signed up, she'd dressed in a loose-fitting pink T-shirt and black tights scavenged from the back of a dresser drawer. Instead of bare feet as the class description suggested, she was wearing heavy cotton socks. It was still wintry, and she didn't like cold feet.

She was struggling with a different kind of cold feet as she peeked into the room. At least she'd worried about the ages of the participants without good reason. The group, mostly women, with a few men in the back row, was mixed in age. She recognized a middle-aged woman who worked the lunch shift at the Cove and several young mothers from church.

A woman in the front row waved at her, and she waved back, surprised to see ninety-five-year-old Maxine Gorman. She had to admire anyone who participated in two exercise classes, but she wondered about how difficult it would be.

She found a place at the rear and was lulled by soft instrumental music, the kind she might use to help herself fall asleep.

The instructor standing at the front of the room was a tall, lithe woman in her midfifties. There were crinkly lines around her friendly blue eyes, and a long gray braid hung down her back. She looked trim and athletic in a black leotard and black footless tights with a flowing flowered skirt. Like most of the women in the room, she was barefoot.

"Welcome to tai chi," the instructor said, shedding her skirt. "I'm Tillie Marsden, and I'll be your guide. We have two newcomers today, I see."

A short perky blonde woman in the second row introduced herself, so Margaret felt she had to do the same.

"I'm Margaret Hoskins," she said a bit self-consciously.

At least the class didn't welcome her in a singsong voice like they did in the SeniorClass. All she wanted was to remain invisible in the back row.

Margaret joined her classmates in standing with feet wide apart, moving her arms at shoulder height for what Tillie Marsden simply called Opening.

"During a tai chi class," she explained, "we go through a series of forms, each one a series of movements, in specific order."

"You'll love the names," the woman next to Margaret told her quietly. "My favorite is White Crane Spreads Its Wings."

"Tai chi improves strength, flexibility, and breathing," Tillie said between directions. "Lower-body moves are especially good for promoting balance in older participants. It also has antihypertensive effects in sedentary older people."

"It makes my joints feel good," the same woman in the front commented.

"I feel so relaxed after tai chi," Maxine said.

Much to her surprise, Margaret didn't find it terribly difficult to follow the instructor's moves. They began with breathing exercises and went through a series of slow to moderate, graceful, flowing poses. Out of the corners of her eyes, she saw her classmates moving in unison with her.

Separating the Clouds was actually fun. Along with the others, Margaret imagined picking up a big fluffy cloud, then turning her palms to push it away in two directions.

In Phoenix Breath, Margaret stood with her feet wide apart, inhaled, raised her arms over her head and exhaled. In her imagination she played with a balloon and rowed a boat in the middle of a lake.

The only form that troubled her involved squats and measured kicks, but she tried her hardest and didn't disgrace herself. No doubt she would master the moves with more practice. She surprised herself by realizing she would return for more tai chi. The slow movements made it possible for her to keep up with the others around her, and Tillie Marsden convinced her about the physical benefits. Continued practice promised a better flow of nutrients and lubricants to the joints and strengthening of the tendons and ligaments. The flowing movements disguised the high number of joint rotations.

"Oh, this helps my arthritis so much," one of the older participants said.

After the class, Margaret was amazed by how she felt. It had been a fairly vigorous workout, something she badly needed, but at the same time it was surprisingly soothing.

"How did it go?" Allan asked when she got home.

"I moved clouds, played with balloons, rode a horse, and rowed a boat in the middle of a lake," she said enthusiastically.

"You did what?" he asked, arching his brows in surprise.

"In my imagination," she said with a smile. "I actually enjoyed it. Now, how's my girl?"

"She went to her room. I think the medication made her sleepy."

"Extra sleep is the best thing for a cold," Margaret said. "Let's hope she'll get over it soon. I think Shelley misses her help as much as Adelaide misses the children. It's a happy arrangement for both of them."

"So you're going to take more tai chi classes?" Allan asked, always one to keep on topic.

"Yes," she told him. "Actually, I can't wait for the next one."

CHAPTER NINETEEN

Diane was beginning to dread answering her phone. She'd followed too many false leads and heard from too many people who knew nothing about Rocky. Tami Harper's tip had been a good one, but unfortunately the golden-haired dog at the school wasn't her beloved pet.

She was beginning to believe Rocky was out of her life forever. Maybe he'd found a new home, possibly even one with children and another dog for companionship. But as hard as she tried to be optimistic, down deep she feared he'd met an untimely end. Even in the relatively rural area around Marble Cove, there were many hazards for a dog on the loose. If he hadn't been hit by a vehicle he might have met a predator like a bear or succumbed to illness.

It was tempting not to answer her phone when it rang Friday morning, but she checked the caller ID and saw Beverly's number.

"Good morning," she said, summoning a cheerful voice in spite of her gloomy mood.

"I was wondering whether you found Rocky," Beverly said after they exchanged pleasantries.

"No, I've almost given up hope, but thanks for asking."

"That's so sad," Beverly commiserated. "I know he means a lot to you."

Diane glanced down at the familiar rawhide bone and wondered whether it was time to throw it away.

"I'm sorry I haven't been more supportive about your job opportunity. I'd hate to see you leave, but you should do what's best for your future." Diane tried to sound upbeat, but she really didn't want to lose a good friend.

"I appreciate hearing that. I've made my decision."

"You're going to take it?" Diane wasn't surprised.

"Yes. It's the kind of offer that comes once in a lifetime. My father is very supportive. He thinks I'd be foolish not to take it."

"Congratulations, Beverly. I really mean it. You have so much talent, and I know Marble Cove doesn't offer many opportunities for a career woman."

"Your understanding means a lot," Beverly said, sounding a little choked up. "I had dinner with Jeff and told him about it. He was very noncommittal. I don't have a clue how he feels."

"You probably took him by surprise." Diane pushed the rawhide with her toe, deciding to put it away so it wouldn't be a constant reminder of Rocky.

"Probably. Anyway, I've been thinking about searching for the treasure with metal detectors. Margaret said Allan tried theirs and it's still working, and Dan just has to fix a broken wire to make his functional. We can set a time to check out the old cemetery, if we're all still together on this," Beverly said.

"I shiver just thinking about it." Her office suddenly seemed cooler to Diane.

"You still want to do it?" Beverly sounded a little doubtful herself.

"Yes, of course. My curiosity won't let me back out." Diane chuckled, knowing her need to discover secrets had led to trouble more than once. "I hope our real-life mystery goes better than my fictional one."

"You're still having trouble with the book?" Beverly sounded genuinely concerned, and Diane appreciated it.

"I can't seem to summon up any enthusiasm. The mystery looks good in my outline, but the characters lack something essential. They feel too cookie-cutter to me. So far, they don't have the spark they need for the reader to be fully involved."

"You had great characters in your first book, at least in the draft I read," Beverly said thoughtfully. "Maybe you just have too much else on your mind."

"Yes, I'm afraid I'll probably need to say good-bye to Rocky and get on with it, although he isn't the cause of my writer's block."

"Could you take a week or two off, maybe visit your daughter?" Beverly suggested. "A break might give you new perspective."

"That's a good idea, but I've dawdled so much, I don't have any time to spare. I take deadlines very seriously. When I was a reporter, stories had to be done on time or they wouldn't be used."

"You'll get your edge back," Beverly assured her. "You have more than enough talent to make the second book even better than the first."

"Thanks. I hope you're right. I've heard of the 'sophomore slump,' but this is getting ridiculous." She paused. "But about the cemetery. When do you want to go?"

"I'm looking at tomorrow night if the weather cooperates," Beverly said. "The prediction is for moderate cold and no precipitation, the best we can hope for this time of year."

"Yes, and then you'll be leaving us the first week in April, won't you?" Diane asked.

"Then or a few days sooner. I hate to leave without a good try at finding Thorpe's treasure. Can I count you in on the hunt?"

"Definitely," Diane said in a firm tone. "I've gone over and over his letters. I'm positive he hid something of value."

"Wouldn't it be wonderful to find something worth enough to finance the renovations at Old First? It would make me feel my time here was worthwhile."

"I'm sure you've enriched a lot of lives while you've been here," Diane assured her.

"I'm not so sure. I love my father, but I don't think he really needs me here. He's getting on very well with Mrs. Peabody to help with meals. He spends most of his time with his books and a few old friends." Beverly sighed.

"He won't consider moving to Chicago with you?" It seemed like a practical solution to Diane, but she also sympathized with Mr. Wheeland. She would hate to move again now that she'd become a part of the Marble Cove community.

"No, he's happy here. He won't even discuss the possibility, but I'm still going to check into assisted living facilities near me. Maybe someday..."

Her words trailed off, and Diane could hear the regret in her voice. Beverly had moved to be near her father. Maybe her sacrifice hadn't worked out as well as she'd hoped.

"I'll pray you find what you're looking for in your new job," Diane said. "And you will keep in touch, won't you?"

"Of course!" Beverly agreed warmly. "That's the great thing about e-mail. We can chat any time we like. I'll want a play-by-play on how the book is going."

"And I can't wait to hear more about your new job. I'm really glad you called. You've reminded me I have to start thinking of the book as my job. If I keep regular hours and don't let myself be distracted, there's no reason why I can't get back on track." Diane tried to sound more optimistic than she felt.

Beverly hung up after promising to get back to her on a time to explore the old cemetery.

Her friend's call did make Diane feel more focused. After all, Beverly had enough confidence in herself to go halfway across the country for a job that might or might not work out well. All Diane had to do was sit at her computer and concentrate on telling a good story. She had the perfect work-at-home scenario, and there was no reason she couldn't get back on her A game.

The pep talk to herself faded as she returned to her computer. She checked her e-mail, looked up a few minor details about her heroine's town on Google, and lost her inspiration. She spent the next hour reading and rereading what she'd written the day before, making minor revisions and checking her spelling and grammar.

Her editor, Jane Veers, and her agent, Frieda Watley, had been making nervous inquiries into her progress, and she'd manage to assuage their concerns, for now. At the rate she was going, the book wouldn't be done until 2020. Even if she had that much time, she doubted it would be as good as the last one. Lots of authors managed to write one great book and never write another. Was she one of them? Was it the pressure of knowing her editor was waiting expectantly, or had she used up her talent on the first book?

It was ironic she'd found faith in God but lost faith in herself. She prayed every day to recover the spark in her writing, or at least to understand what was holding her back.

After doing all she could on her chapter, she saved her work and put the computer to sleep. Although she wasn't particularly hungry, she decided to make lunch. Sometimes ideas came to her when she was doing something unrelated to writing.

The fridge was pretty empty, but she found a partial brick of sharp cheddar cheese and sliced it to make a toasted sandwich. She was in the mood for something sharp and tasty, so she added her favorite mustard, buttered the outsides of the bread, and popped the sandwich under her oven broiler.

She'd just turned it to toast the second side when the phone sounded in her office. Without thinking, she hurried to pick it up before it stopped ringing. Maybe it was Beverly calling back with a time to meet for their treasure hunt.

"Hi," she said, summoning her most chipper voice and expecting to hear her friend's voice.

"Are you the person who put up the posters about a missing dog?" a hesitant female voice asked.

"Yes, I'm Diane Spencer."

"I'm Gina Foster. My husband Ted and I live on a tree farm about twelve miles from Marble Cove. I think we may have your retriever/Lab mix."

Diane was torn between hope and fear of being disappointed again.

"Where did you find him?" she asked a bit breathlessly.

"He was wandering along the county road near our place," Gina said. "He wasn't wearing a collar, but we could tell right away he's a good-tempered dog. He hopped right into our pickup when Ted whistled for him. We thought it would be a shame to take him to a pet shelter."

"When did you find him? That's a long way for him to go," Diane asked, worried this was another false lead.

"What day was it?" the caller asked someone on her end. "We've had him about a week," she told Diane. "How long has your dog been missing?"

"About two weeks."

"I guess that would explain why he was so dirty and hungry when we found him," the caller said.

"It was so nice of you to take him in," Diane said, allowing herself to hope a little.

"Oh, we love dogs! We have three of our own, two black Labs and a collie. Charlie Chaplin made friends with Mary Pickford and Rudolph Valentino right away. Douglas Fairbanks was a little standoffish, but he's getting up in years and doesn't play well with others."

"You name your dogs after old movie stars?"

"Yeah, we love silent films. Of course, we shortened the names to Picky, Rudy, and Dougy. We called your dog—if he is your dog—Charlie."

"Would it be all right if I come to your place and see him?" Diane asked.

"Oh, you don't need to go to the trouble. We have to make a trip to Marble Cove this afternoon anyway. We'll bring him in."

"I would appreciate it so much," Diane said, giving them directions to find her cottage.

"See you in an hour or so," her caller said, then paused. "I kinda hope Charlie isn't yours, we've taken to him so much, but I know how attached a person can get to a good dog."

As soon as Diane hung up, she smelled burning. She raced to the kitchen and pulled a square of smoking charcoal from the broiler, all that was left of her sandwich.

How could she be so absentminded! Of course, if she hadn't hurried to answer the phone, she might have missed a chance to recover Rocky—if the caller did actually have him.

She was much too excited to fix anything else for lunch, but she kept cautioning herself not to get carried away. Mainers loved dogs, and there were a lot of them in the area. How Rocky had wandered—or been taken—that far would be one more unsolved mystery.

By the time her front doorbell rang, she was pacing with anticipation. She opened it before the chimes died away.

"Ms. Spencer?" a tall, angular woman in her early forties asked.

"Yes, have you brought the dog?" She didn't want to jinx a possible reunion by using his name.

"Should I bring him inside? Some folks are particular about dogs in the house."

"Yes, of course!" Diane tried to peer around the smiling face of the pale blonde woman. "No, I can't wait. I'll go outside to see him."

She hurried out, not even noticing the chilly wind in her haste to check out the dog huddled in the rear of an old green pickup.

"Rocky!"

She knew the instant she saw him. He stood in the bed of the truck on a pile of old blankets, his tail waving like a weathervane in a hurricane. Mrs. Foster lowered the tailgate, and Rocky bounded into Diane's arms, nearly knocking her off her feet.

"I let him borrow one of Rudy's old collars so he wouldn't get away from me," his "foster" mother said.

"I can't thank you enough for rescuing him," Diane said. "Please come inside."

"I have to meet my husband at Dr. Spangler's. Our Douglas Fairbanks cut his leg on a piece of wire fencing. We thought we'd best have the vet look at it," she said. "I'll just step in to get Rudy's collar back. We'll miss him, but I'm glad he's home."

Once inside the door, Diane stooped to hug her errant pet, not at all bothered when he slobbered kisses on her face. She unfastened the borrowed collar and handed it to his benefactor.

"Wait just a minute. I have the reward ready for you," Diane said, hurrying to a bookshelf where she'd put the cash in an envelope when she first put out posters.

The woman made a dismissive gesture. "Ted and I don't need a reward. We'd do the same for any stray we found along the road."

"I promised it on the poster, and I need to give it to you. You have no idea how happy I am to get Rocky back. He looks wonderful! His coat is gorgeous. You must have brushed him before you came."

"I know just how happy you are. My dogs are like my children, so naturally I bathed and groomed him for the homecoming. I like my dogs to look sharp," Mrs. Foster said.

"He looks fantastic!" Diane said, handling over the reward. "I don't have words to thank you."

"Your smile says it all," she said. "Thank you for the reward. I have to get to the vet's now."

Rocky showed no inclination to dash out the door with his rescuer.

"What should I say to my naughty runaway?" Diane asked, kneeling to hug and pet him. "I guess 'welcome home' says it all."

After lunch and a long one-sided conversation with Rocky, she went back to her office. He trailed after her and wasted no time locating his rawhide and settling down in his accustomed place to watch her work.

After calling her friends to tell them the good news about Rocky, she opened her chapter and realized she had to go back to the beginning of the book. Now she knew exactly what was missing from her story—and how to fix it.

"Well, Rocky," she said with a broad grin. "You're about to go down in literary history. No good detective should be without a canine companion."

CHAPTER TWENTY

In her morning prayers Friday, Margaret had taken stock of the many blessings in her life. She was thankful Adelaide was recovering from her cold, although she still wasn't up to helping Shelley with the children.

She was grateful for finding the tai chi class because she badly wanted to stay healthy as long as possible for her daughter. As always, her marriage to Allan was a constant source of blessings, and now she included her friendships to the list of things greatly enriching her life.

Later that day when she went to the kitchen for lunch, Allan noticed her upbeat mood and commented on it.

"You look happy today," he said, turning a grilled cheese sandwich on the skillet. "I told Adelaide we'd have her favorite for lunch, but she's playing with the cats. I'll have to pull her away soon."

"She and those cats are inseparable," Margaret said.

"Do you have anything else planned for today?" Allan asked. "I'd like to check out the Mercantile. I think they have some drawer pulls I can use on the dresser I'm making. I need something old-fashioned looking."

"They probably have some that have been in stock for fifty years," she said, laughing at the store's reputation for slow-selling merchandise. "I guess Adelaide shouldn't go with you, though. It won't hurt to keep her in another day."

Allan put a sandwich on her plate and sat with her to say a blessing.

"So what are you going to do with the rest of your day?" he asked again.

"I'm going to try to lay out the artwork for the new line of merchandise Matt Beauregard is starting. I haven't been able to get inspired until now, but I woke up this morning with ideas bouncing through my brain."

"Maybe the tai chi stimulated your imagination," her husband said, breaking off a bite of the gooey cheese sandwich with his hands.

"You could be right. I'm finally shaking off the winter blahs."

Later, when Margaret was sketching a possible scene of the lighthouse with an old sailing boat in the distance, her phone rang. She was so hard at work that she was tempted to ignore it, but something told her to answer.

"Margaret," Beverly said, "are you still up for some treasure hunting?"

"Sure. And Allan says our metal detector is working fine. When do you want to go?"

"Tomorrow night, late enough to be sure no one will be at the church to see us. I know it's still cold, but I'm accepting the Chicago job. I want to do this before I leave."

"Oh dear, I will miss you," Margaret said, "but I'm so happy for your sake. It sounds like a wonderful opportunity."

"I'm going to miss all of you terribly," Beverly said, "but even my father agrees it's an opportunity I shouldn't pass up."

"Well, I wish you all the luck in the world," Margaret said. "What time should we meet for our treasure hunt?"

"I thought everyone could meet at Diane's house at eleven. We'll go in my car and park a block or so from the cemetery."

"So no one notices we're there," Margaret said with a shiver of excitement. "I used to love beachcombing with the detector, but this tops anything Allan and I did. Do you really think we'll find something?"

"If there's any kind of trunk or box with metal fittings, we have a chance," Beverly said. "For now, though, I'm going to tell my dad we're having a get-together at Diane's. He'll be in bed long before I leave. Loving history as he does, he'd think it was a great lark, but I'd rather Mrs. Peabody doesn't know about it. She's not known for keeping secrets."

"Good idea. We don't want the whole town digging up the graveyard. As it is, we'll have to be very careful not to disturb anything. I have a feeling that Reverend Locke isn't exactly going to be an advocate of treasure hunting," Margaret said.

"He probably won't, although I don't know why he should object to looking for something that could finance the church renovations," Beverly said.

"Maybe we should have shown him the letters, but it seemed like his mind was closed to their potential. He'd

probably tuck them away where no one could read them."
Margaret had known Silas Locke any number of years, and
she was puzzled by his negative attitude.

"It's odd," Beverly agreed. "I just don't understand.
He's such a conscientious and concerned minister. Well, I
still have to call Shelley, so I'd better let you go. See you
tomorrow night."

★   ★   ★

Shelley was in her kitchen watching with awe as Tami finished
filling delicate cream puffs with luscious vanilla custard.
They were destined to go to a Friends of the Library annual
dinner that evening, and all that remained to be done was
top them with a chocolate ganache icing.

"Cream puffs really aren't hard to make," Tami said as
she worked. "The trick is to get them to puff up and stay
puffed. You have to be sure to cool the flour, water, and
butter mixture before putting in the eggs. You don't want
the eggs to get too hot or they won't puff up nicely."

Shelley felt like a rank beginner as Tami went through the
steps to make perfect puff pastry. In truth, she never would
have suggested such a delicate dessert for the library dinner.
There were too many possible mistakes, and she didn't have
the confidence to make perfectly shaped pastry with wet
fingertips the way Tami was doing.

She couldn't fault Tami for her enthusiasm and expertise,
but she had to look ahead to the time her assistant would

leave. How could Shelley possibly live up to the high standards of a soon-to-be New York pastry chef? If the cream puffs were a big success, would other groups order them? If they did, could she supply them on her own?

"They're lovely," Shelley said, a bit awestruck by the tray of perfect pastries.

"Puff pastry really isn't hard," Tami assured her again, icing them with a flourish. "We learned to do it my first term at school."

Shelley felt in over her head. When she'd started her business, she'd been confident in her ability to bake delicious cookies, but in order to expand, she had to make what customers wanted. If her customers got used to Tami's fancy pastries, what would happen to Shelley's business after she left?

The phone was a welcome interruption, and hearing Beverly's voice was a relief. She still had a birthday cake to make for tomorrow and an order of cookies for the Cove. Much as she appreciated the business, she also needed a little downtime. Laundry had piled up again, and Adelaide still wasn't well enough to watch the children. Dan had taken them to his mother's again, a measure Shelley preferred to reserve for emergencies.

"The treasure hunt is on for tomorrow night," Beverly said. "Will you be able to make it?"

"Yes, as long as it's after the kids are in bed. Dan doesn't mind sitting with them, but I've relied on him too much this week. He's trying to study some book on electrical circuits or something, so he won't mind if I leave—as long as the children are asleep."

"We're meeting at Diane's at eleven. There shouldn't be anyone around the church at that time. I know it's still cold, but I'll be leaving at the end of the month to move to Chicago for the new job."

Shelley was surprised by how sad Beverly's news made her feel.

"Congratulations, but I'll really miss you." She glanced over at Tami and decided not to say anything about their plan in front of her. All four friends agreed it would be a bad thing to get the whole town excited about the possibility of a buried treasure.

"Thanks," Beverly said. "Is your metal detector working yet? Margaret will bring hers, but it will go faster with two."

"Dan had to rewire it, but he said it works fine now."

"Great! I'll see you tomorrow."

Saturday morning Shelley wasn't sure how she felt about going to the old cemetery at night. She wouldn't be alone, of course, but it still seemed kind of scary. She'd explored the decommissioned lighthouse with her friends in the daytime, but things seemed more menacing in the dark.

Dan wasn't keen on having her go, but he was a good sport about taking her to the garage and explaining how to use the metal detector while the kids took their afternoon naps.

"Are you sure you want to do this?" he asked as he propped it against the garage door for her to take later.

"Not so much," she admitted, "but I told the others I would."

Late that evening Shelley dressed in her warmest jacket, a knit cap, and sweatpants with leggings under them. The weather had been bleak all day with drizzling rain in the afternoon. She didn't kid herself: it was going to be miserable in the cemetery. After pulling on her rubber boots and a lined pair of gloves, she grabbed the detector and walked across the street to Diane's.

Even though she was a few minutes early, the others had already gathered. Margaret looked lost in Allan's old navy surplus peacoat, and Diane looked twice her size in layers of clothing. Only Beverly managed to look stylish in a hooded jacket and form-fitting ski pants. They all had rubber boots. The cemetery would probably be muddy, so they'd have to be careful not to trample the soft ground.

"When we get there," Beverly said, speaking softly as though practicing for their stealthy mission, "we'll work in teams of two. I'll hold the flashlight for Margaret, and Diane will do the same for you, Shelley. Did everyone bring a little spade for digging?"

"No, I forgot," Shelley admitted, "but I brought a canvas bag in case we find anything."

"No problem," Diane said. "I have my garden spade."

"Then we're ready," Beverly said. "If you have your cell phones with you, we'd better turn them off. The quieter we are, the better." She took her own out of her pocket and made sure the ringer was off.

They all got in Margaret's car to go the short distance to the cemetery. They parked a block away from the church and walked to the ancient graveyard behind it. The area had been fenced to discourage hikers and bikers from using it as a shortcut, but it was easy to step over the low iron barricade. In the summer the gravestones attracted artisans who used rice paper and charcoal to get an image of the primitive art and inscriptions on the seventeenth- and eighteenth-century markers. It wasn't a hobby Shelley had ever wanted to pursue.

Except for a dim nightlight in the church parking lot, the area was shrouded in darkness. They walked beyond that small but comforting illumination into the totally black confines of the cemetery. The sky had been overcast all day, and the moon was still hidden. They only had their flashlights to show them the way.

"I thought one team could begin on the south side and the other on the north. That way we should get the best possible coverage," Beverly said.

Shelley could barely tell up from down, let alone north from south, in the dense darkness. Her teeth were chattering, whether from the cold or from fear she wasn't sure. She clenched her jaws together, hoping the others couldn't hear.

"We'll take the north," Diane said, offering to begin at the far end of the cemetery.

Shelley followed the circle of light from her friend's flashlight, although it hardly seemed to penetrate the enveloping darkness. She'd gone over and over Dan's instructions on how to use the metal detector, but she hadn't practiced in the dark wearing thick gloves. Her fingers felt like sausages as she tried to activate it.

If Diane hadn't been with her, lighting the way and encouraging her, she would've bolted. After a few false starts, they fell into a rhythm, slowly covering the ground between grave markers. The burials were done in rows, but it was treacherous moving down them. A few markers had fallen, blocking the way, and others tilted at odd angles. Worse, the ground underfoot was uneven, and melting snow had dug out channels and pits in the soggy pathway.

They could only walk single file, and Shelley had to lead the way with the detector. Her heart was pounding, and only Diane's presence and calm voice kept her from running back to the car.

"Oh dear!" Diane called out behind her in a stage whisper.

"Are you all right?" Shelley whispered, too unnerved to speak aloud.

"I just stumbled. I'm okay," her friend assured her. Just then the metal detector made a whining noise. "I think you've found something!"

Shelley held the flashlight while Diane carefully removed a scoop of muddy earth and grass. "I have to be careful to replace it exactly as it is," she said more to herself than Shelley. "Yes, here it is."

They both sighed with disappointment when the dim light revealed a rusty barrette, similar to ones Shelley had worn as a kid. In the distance a foghorn seemed to mock them, adding to the unsettling atmosphere in the graveyard.

"I guess we can bury that again," Shelley said.

"At least we know your metal detector is sensitive to small bits of metal. If Jeremiah Thorpe buried a trunk, some of the metal could've rusted away."

Shelley nearly stumbled over a fallen gravestone, and something dark streaked in front of her. She squealed and backed into Diane, almost knocking both of them off their feet.

"A cat," Diane said with a relieved laugh.

"I've never been so scared in my life," Shelley said, wanting nothing more than to bolt for home.

"Well," Diane said. "This seemed like a good idea when we were sitting in a warm, well-lit house. I never realized how creepy this place is, but then I've never been here at night."

"And I never will be again!" Shelley said, still trembling from the feline encounter.

"Here," Diane said. "Why don't you take the flashlight and I'll try running the metal detector."

Shelley shone the flashlight on the wet ground and Diane slowly swept the heavy machine from side to side. An unearthly squeal pierced the darkness, and Shelley jumped. "Must be something big!" she whispered.

Diane handed Shelley the garden spade and she began digging, rueful of the mess that it would leave behind them. She hoped they'd be able to patch it over so it wasn't obvious that they'd been there.

After a few moments of carefully scooping the dirt and roots away, Shelley heard the spade make a scraping sound. Shelley stopped and peered excitedly at Diane. "What do you think it is?"

Shelley began gingerly brushing away the remaining dirt, and Diane knelt to help her. A rectangular outline about five or six inches wide and perhaps a foot long revealed itself in their narrow flashlight beam. Diane dug her fingers deeper into the soil around the object, trying to find the bottom. To her disappointment, she didn't have to dig deep. She pried the metal object from the mud, brushed it off, and held it up to Shelley. In the gleam of the flashlight, Shelley could now make out the block lettering against a faded yellow background. "'Maine. 68. Vacationland,'" she read. "A *license plate?*"

Shelley began laughing silently, and Diane joined in. They decided to take it with them. "People collect these, you know," Diane whispered to her. "And besides, someone could trip on it."

A dim circle of light from Beverly's flashlight was moving closer as they approached their meeting point. Shelley's feet were so cold she could hardly feel them, and Diane had to stop repeatedly to massage feeling back into her fingers. Running the detector over the uneven ground was hard on Shelley's back, and Diane's gloves were thick with mud.

Shelley tried to focus on the task, but her imagination was running wild. Who were all these poor souls under the frigid ground? Had they enjoyed long, happy lives, or had they been snatched from life before they even experienced it? She knew from a summer stroll through the cemetery that many babies died at birth and were laid beside the mothers who gave up their lives bringing them into the world. She thanked the Lord for the life she lived and prayed for those who hadn't been as fortunate.

"Wait!" Diane whispered urgently, suddenly turning off her flashlight.

Shelley froze, ripples of fear coursing down her spine. She wished herself safely home, tucked into bed under a warm quilt.

"You have no right to be here," a harsh male voice boomed, coming from several rows over where Beverly and Margaret were searching.

"Reverend Silas Locke," Diane whispered. "We're busted, but what on earth is *he* doing here at this hour?"

Shelley's first instinct was to duck down behind a tombstone, but loyalty to her friends forbade hiding. Diane must have been thinking the same thing because she turned on the flashlight and slowly made her way toward the small group.

"I'm disappointed in you, Beverly," the minister was saying, singling out the lone member of his own congregation among the group. "Breaking through the ceiling of the church was bad enough. Just what do you think you're doing here in the middle of the night?"

"We hoped to find something to help with the church repairs," Beverly said, never one to back down. "We're not hurting anything."

"If what you're doing is so innocent, why are you tramping across hallowed ground in the middle of the night?"

No one had an answer, but he didn't expect one.

"This foolishness has to stop. Can you imagine what would happen to this historic cemetery if everyone in town got wind of possible treasure? I absolutely forbid you access to this burial ground. It's church property, and I won't tolerate trespassing. I won't call the authorities and press charges this time," he said, shaking a gloved finger, "but do not let it happen again."

Shelley had never heard a man of God speak so harshly, and she froze where she stood.

He strode away without a backward glance, and Shelley followed the others out of the cemetery a few moments later. They didn't talk on the way back to Diane's, where they had to leave their boots and tools outside because they were so muddy.

"I guess the least I can do is offer you some tea," Diane said in a discouraged voice as they filed into her small front room.

They gathered around her kitchen table and sipped the hot brew. Shelley gradually warmed up enough to take off her coat.

"Did you find anything?" Margaret asked, still rubbing her hands to restore circulation.

"Just a nail and a barrette," Shelley unhappily admitted. "And an old license plate." She laughed as she held it up for the others to see. "Boy, we thought we'd really found something too! We brought it back so it wouldn't trip someone. How about you?"

"We found an old half dollar for our trouble," Margaret said, digging a coin out of her pocket and handing it to Beverly. "You can put it in the collection plate Sunday."

"If it's silver, it might buy a few nails for the renovation," Beverly said with an ironic smile. "I'm sure we looked silly to Reverend Locke out there tonight, but I don't know why he is so fanatically opposed to looking into the past."

"Wait a minute," Diane said. "Did anyone else notice that Reverend Locke mentioned buried treasure? None of us said anything about treasure! What do you think he knows?"

"You're right, Diane," Beverly agreed. "Do you think it's possible he knows about the treasure and is trying to keep us from finding it before he does?"

"Now, now," Margaret said. "I think your imaginations might be getting the better of you. Do you really think a minister would try to hide something that could save his own church?"

"I don't know," replied Shelley. "But it sure seems suspicious to me."

"Well, at the very least he has a point about being in the cemetery," Diane said unhappily. "I hope we didn't make a mess of the ground between the stones by walking there."

"Not likely," Beverly said. "The ground is always pitted and rough. We didn't do any damage."

"But why was he there? It's after midnight," Shelley asked.

"Before you came, he said he always goes to the church to pray when he feels the need for it. Apparently he's a night owl," Beverly said. "I'm sorry I got you all into this."

"We all wanted to go," Margaret assured her. "You still believe Jeremiah Thorpe hid something of value, don't you?"

Beverly nodded.

Shelley joined the others in giving assent. "Yes. But what do we do now?"

Chapter Twenty-One

Beverly stared in puzzlement when she returned home from the unsuccessful treasure hunt. There were way too many lights showing through the first-floor windows of her father's old Victorian house. He was good about leaving the porch light on when she was out in the evening, but it was unlike him to keep the whole house lit up like a Christmas tree. He was, by nature, a thrifty New Englander.

Alarm bells went off in Beverly's head. She hurried up the flagstone walkway, nearly slipping because the frigid temperature had made the cold drizzle treacherous. Even more surprising, the solid wooden front door was open a crack. One of the first things her father had taught her as a child was to shut the door in winter so the "good" air wouldn't get out.

As soon as she stepped into the front room, Mrs. Peabody hurried toward her from the kitchen. She was wearing a pink fleece housecoat with only the tips of her fingers and the toes of her bedroom slippers showing. The only possible reason for the older woman to be there in the middle of the night was because something had happened to her father, something bad. When Beverly noticed some dark stains on the front of her robe, her anxiety escalated.

"I'm so glad you're here," the older woman said. "I didn't know whether to go in the ambulance or go home or stay here."

"Ambulance? What happened?" Beverly dreaded the answer.

"Your father had a fall. I'm only guessing, but he probably needed to use the necessary room. Most old folks get up at least once..."

"Please," Beverly interrupted, too panicked to wait for a long explanation. "Is my father okay?"

"I wouldn't say 'okay.' They took him to the hospital in an ambulance. I don't think he was badly hurt, but the paramedics thought he should be checked."

"How did you happen to be here?"

"He called me when he couldn't get you. Said he didn't think a little fall warranted 911."

Beverly remembered turning off her cell phone so it wouldn't ring in the cemetery. How could she have forgotten to turn it on again? She dug it out of her pocket and turned it on, but there was no message, only notice of several missed calls.

Beverly was so upset she was trembling, and she wanted to get to the hospital as soon as possible.

"Thank you so much for staying here to tell me," she said.

"The Mister made me promise to wait until you got here. Can you drive me home? I don't want to traipse back in my nightie too."

"No, of course not," Beverly said, quickly offering to drive her home. "Do you have any idea why he fell?"

"You'll know when you get to be my age. Sometimes us old folks just lose our balance and topple over for no good reason. I don't think he broke his hip though. That would be—"

"Do you have a coat?" Beverly interrupted. She didn't mean to be rude, but she was far too distracted to pay attention to Mrs. Peabody's rambling. "I'll drop you at home on my way to the hospital."

"No, just my nice warm robe. Not as if it's January out there. I've seen it a whole lot colder in March."

"I really need to leave now," Beverly insisted.

"Well, just let me douse the lights." The older woman turned. "The Mister doesn't like to waste the electricity."

"Mrs. Peabody!" Beverly said sharply. "Please. The lights don't matter. Now, my car is in front. Give me your arm so you don't slip."

She propelled the birdlike elderly woman toward her car as quickly as possible.

"These flagstones are a tad slippery," Mrs. Peabody complained.

By the time she got Mrs. Peabody settled in the car and out again at her house, Beverly was frantic to get to Sailors Memorial hospital just outside of town. She paused only to confirm her phone was on, then drove there as fast as possible without breaking any traffic laws.

The sleepy-eyed young man on duty at the hospital reception desk checked on her father's whereabouts for her.

"He's been moved to room 210," he said stifling a yawn. "You can go on up. The elevator is—"

"Yes, I know where it is. Thank you," she said, hurrying to see him.

How badly was her father hurt? Obviously his fall was serious enough to keep him overnight, but she was more worried about the cause of his fall than possible injury. Not so very long ago he'd had a series of ministrokes the doctor called TIA's. They caused sporadic memory loss and confusion, but the medication he was taking to prevent them had seemed to be working. Lately he'd been cheerful and busy with his books. Had another TIA caused him to fall?

She stepped out of the elevator into the hushed atmosphere of a hospital corridor. A lone nurse was working at the nurses' station, and Beverly hurried over to ask permission to see her father. Her instinct was to run down the hallway in search of his room, but she knew hospitals had rules about visitors. Much to her relief, the nurse was friendly and reassuring.

"You're welcome to look in on him," she said. "He was still awake last time I checked, but he's been given a sedative to help him sleep."

Beverly found the room and paused for a few anxious seconds before stepping through the open doorway.

"Father? Are you all right?" she asked as she approached the high hospital bed in the faint light coming from the corridor. "Of course you aren't, or you wouldn't be here. You gave me such a scare."

She realized she was babbling, and she wasn't reassured by a stark white bandage across his forehead.

"Your head…"

"Just a little cut. Head wounds bleed like a water faucet, but mine isn't serious. Not as if I broke anything."

Beverly sat on the edge of the bed beside him, not caring whether she broke every hospital rule in the book. She gingerly took his hand, being careful not to dislodge an IV drip.

"I'm so sorry my phone was off."

"What's done is done. How did the grave robbing go?" he asked with a trace of humor.

"Reverend Locke caught us. He was less than pleased. But I want to know what happened to you. Was it another little stroke?"

"No, just an old man with two left feet. I fell asleep in my recliner. When I woke up suddenly, I started to get up but tripped on that old afghan I had on my lap. Happened so quick, it felt like flying. Silly thing was, I couldn't get up again. Never heard of such a thing—a grown man stuck on the floor. Lucky I could crawl to the phone."

"Yes, we both owe Mrs. Peabody a big thank-you."

"Thanks for nothing," he said sounding more like himself in his irritation. "I told that woman not to call 911. All I needed was help getting up. She got all panicky over a little blood. Are you here to take me home?"

"I don't think you can check out of the hospital in the middle of the night," Beverly said sympathetically, lightly squeezing his hand. "Why don't you try sleeping, and we'll see what the doctor says in the morning."

"He'll say they have to run tests," her father grumbled. "That's what docs always say. How do you think hospitals make their money?"

"We'll sort it out in the morning," Beverly assured him. "Why don't you try to get some sleep now?"

"A man sleeps better in his own house," he said, beginning to sound a little drowsy. His eyelids drooped.

"I'm so happy it was just a minor accident. I worry about you."

He opened his eyes and looked intently at her. "Now don't be using this as an excuse not to take the job in Chicago. I had a little accident, is all, and I handled it without you."

"You did well. We'll talk about the job tomorrow."

Beverly pulled the room's only chair closer to the bed and watched while he nodded off. Her father was in good hands. Maybe there was no reason to stay, but she couldn't bring herself to leave. She needed to hear his even breathing and watch his still form, even if he didn't know she was still watching over him.

In the silence of the night she prayed for his recovery and for guidance in making the right decision about leaving him.

Later, much later, she dozed, but when she awoke at dawn, she knew what she was going to do. She loved her father too much to desert him. She had lost sight of the very thing that had brought her to Marble Cove. She hoped her father had many good years left, but his accident reminded her that there was no guarantee of that.

She watched him sleep until a nurse in purple flowered scrubs came into the room to check his vitals. It took her father a few moments to realize Beverly was still in his room.

"Don't tell me you camped out here all night?" he said with mock severity.

"I fell asleep in the chair," she equivocated. "Guess I was too sleepy to drive home."

"Speaking of which, when are we going there?" he asked, watching without interest as the nurse took his blood pressure. "Can you get me signed out of here?" he asked the nurse.

"Sorry, the doctor will have to do that, but he'll be along sometime after breakfast."

"I know how doctors operate. It could be dinnertime before he gets here." He said it matter-of-factly, and Beverly suspected he needed time to get his bearings. "You might as well go home, but leave your phone on. I'll call you when I can get out of here."

"If you're sure you don't mind..."

"You're not too old to do what your father says once in a while," he said with the customary twinkle in his eye. "And tell that woman we'll buy her a new robe. She'll never get the blood out of hers."

"That's sweet of you, Father," Beverly said. "I will go home and change out of my graveyard clothes, but I'll be waiting for your call."

Beverly drove home slowly, still shaken by the events of the previous evening. She'd alienated the minister of her newfound church, but she also felt closer to her father than she had in many years. Most importantly, she felt God had given her the wisdom she'd been praying for to make the right decision about leaving Marble Cove. Now that she'd decided to stay, the faraway job seemed pointless and uninteresting. If she'd learned one thing from her father's fall, it was to recognize that nothing mattered to her as much as he did.

She smiled when she thought of telling him she was staying. He would argue and try to be self-sacrificing, but in his heart he would be as happy as she was now.

He called in midafternoon, grumbling because the doctor had taken so long to sign him out.

"It is Sunday," Beverly said as they drove home. "I imagine even doctors need some time off on the weekend."

"Lucky for me it's too cold for golf. I'd still be sitting there."

Her father looked rakish with his forehead bandaged under the felt hat she'd brought for him to wear home. Maybe he was a little pale, but he didn't show any other visible signs of trauma from his fall.

She waited until he was settled in his recliner to talk about Chicago.

"Isn't it time for you to start packing?" he asked. "You'll need some time to look for a place to stay before you start the new job."

"No, I won't," she said firmly.

"You won't? You're not backing off because of me, are you? You know I won't stand in the way of a good opportunity."

She didn't know whether he was relieved or irritated. Sometimes his flat Maine accent made it hard to read his emotions. She walked over to him and put her arms around his shoulders.

"Father, I'm staying with you here in Marble Cove. It's my final decision."

His eyes watered, and he wiped them on the sleeve of the plaid flannel shirt she'd brought to the hospital for him to wear.

"You're sure you won't regret it ten minutes from now?" he asked in a subdued voice.

"I won't regret staying here with you ten years from now. I have a home here, and it's with you."

He smiled at her and patted her hand. "You're a good daughter, Beverly."

Her father went to bed early in his own room that evening, more exhausted from his accident than he was willing to admit. When she was sure he was sleeping comfortably, Beverly checked her e-mails for the day. One stood out.

"Hi, Beverly: I'm really sorry you'll be moving to Chicago. I'll make sure we'll still see each other, but I'm afraid it will be a little tricky to get to Chicago as often as I'd like. Will you have time to see me before you leave? Anything I can do to help you pack? Best of luck! Jeff."

She made her answer short and sweet.

"Jeff, good news! At least I hope you think so. I'm turning down the Chicago job. I'll explain when I see you. Thanks for your offer to help. I won't need a rain check on that. Beverly."

Her Marble Cove friends might be in bed, but she couldn't wait to share her news. She sent a message to Diane, knowing she checked her e-mail frequently.

"Hi, friend: I won't be going to Chicago. I'll explain when I see you. Maybe we can take another look at Thorpe's letters sometime soon. I'll try to make nice with Reverend Locke after church next week, but I'm not optimistic. At least I know he's too staunch a man of God to want me out of his congregation. Call me when you have time! Take care, Beverly."

She was much too tired after the restless night at the hospital to stay awake long, but she thanked the Lord for the realization her father was far more important than any job.

Before she closed her eyes for the night, Beverly wondered whether they would ever get to the bottom of Marble Cove's mysterious past.

She couldn't wait to try.

CHAPTER TWENTY-TWO

Mama, do I have to go to Meemaw's today?" Aiden was dawdling over his bowl of oatmeal Monday morning, getting as much on the front of his pajamas as he did in his mouth.

"No, Adelaide is feeling better. She'll be here pretty soon, so please finish your breakfast. It would be nice if you dressed yourself before she gets here."

"I wanna wear my space shirt."

"Your red shirt isn't clean. You'll have to wear your blue one. I laid it out on your bed."

Emma picked that moment to bang on the tray of her high chair, flipping her spoon and knocking a blob of oatmeal to the floor.

"Gotta head out," Dan said, poking his head into the dining area where his breakfast dishes were still on the table.

Shelley sighed in frustration. He had to see a man about a possible part-time job, but she wished he could help with the children for a few minutes. She had a lot of baking to do, but at least Tami was coming to help her.

She wiped up the floor, cleaned Emma's face, and shooed Aiden to his room to get dressed. The table had to be cleared and the breakfast dishes put in the dishwasher. She was fresh out of the starched white chef jackets, but ordering another was out of the question.

Half an hour later, Adelaide was happily entertaining the children, and Shelley had managed to brush her teeth before beginning work. As Mondays went, it wasn't the worst start she'd had. Oddly though, Tami wasn't there yet. She was more likely to be early than late, so Shelley hoped nothing had happened to delay her.

Besides her usual order from the Cove, she had to bake cookies for a big bridal shower the next evening. It was a chance to show she could do fancy treats for special occasions. Tami had helped decide what to offer, and now Shelley was obligated to provide two things she'd never tried before. She liked to practice a recipe before selling it, but Tami had convinced her to skip that precaution.

She read the two new recipes, frowning at the use of two ingredients new to her. The first, almond macaroons, called for almond paste. The second recipe called for sunflower seeds, something Shelley thought of as food to put on winter bird feeders. The bride was into health foods, and Tami had hit on a cookie made with whole-wheat flour and sunflower seeds. Shelley could only cross her fingers on that idea.

She started assembling the ingredients and entering oven times and temperatures on the chart Tami had taught her to use. It was a good idea, she had to admit, and so was the notepad with a running list of things she needed to buy. Sometimes her helper pushed her to try things beyond her comfort zone, but Shelley couldn't fault her for the way she organized the kitchen.

It was nearly ten, and Tami still wasn't there. Shelley delayed starting the macaroons, sure they would turn out better if Tami made them. When the phone rang, she had a bad feeling about answering it.

"It's Tami," her helper said. "You won't believe what I did yesterday. I slipped carrying some things down the basement stairs for my mother. My ankle swelled up like a balloon, and she insisted I see a doctor first thing this morning."

"Are you all right?" Shelley asked with concern.

"Well, I didn't break anything, but I have a badly sprained ankle. I should have called sooner. The doctor said I have to use crutches and stay off it, probably for the rest of the week. That means I won't be able to help you anymore. I'm so sorry."

"Don't worry, I'll get by fine," Shelley assured her, trying to sound as upbeat as possible. "The important thing is for you to rest your ankle."

"I would look like a klutz if I showed up in class on crutches," Tami said with a forced laugh. "But I'm sorry to let you down."

"I'll be fine," Shelley said, although the butterflies in her stomach told her otherwise. "You take care of yourself. I can't thank you enough for all the help you've given me."

"You don't need to thank me. I enjoyed every minute."

"Well, take care," Shelley said, ending the conversation.

She made herself a cup of tea, set it aside, and forgot to drink it. She checked the kids, and, of course, they were having a good time with Adelaide. Then, to be sure she was ready to start the new recipe for almond macaroons, she reread it three times, trying to be sure she wouldn't make any mistakes.

For the rest of the morning, she worked with dogged determination. She was an experienced baker. There was no reason to be thrown by a new recipe, however difficult it looked on paper. Tami had shown her how to handle fancy pastry, and she had to admit her baked goods looked more polished and professional than they used to.

When Margaret came to pick up her daughter a little before two, both children were taking a nap at the same time, a minor miracle, and she had time to visit with her friend.

"So, have you recovered from our graveyard adventure?" Margaret asked.

"It's not something I want to repeat," Shelley admitted with a giggle. "I hope Reverend Locke isn't too angry with Beverly."

"I think our Beverly can hold her own with anyone," Margaret said. "And isn't it wonderful she isn't going to Chicago?"

"Yes, when I got her text first thing this morning, I danced with joy—well, at least in my head. And I wanted to tell you how happy I am to have Adelaide back."

"She couldn't wait to get here."

"As you can see," Shelley said, pointing to cooling racks full of cookies, "I really needed her today. Tami sprained her ankle and couldn't come."

"I'm sure you'll get along fine without Tami," Margaret said. "After all, you've built your business from scratch all on your own. The way you're going, you'll be baking for the whole town. Maybe then you can hire a helper."

"That's still a ways in the future," Shelley said with a pleased grin.

After Margaret and Adelaide left, Shelley looked with satisfaction at her day's output. The macaroons were golden brown and luscious looking, certainly nice enough for any bride's shower. The sunflower cookies tasted much better than she'd expected, and they hadn't given her any trouble. She had Tami to thank for today's success.

There had been times when Tami tried her patience by throwing new ideas and techniques at her faster than she could absorb them, but she'd been wrong to be intimidated by her helper's skills.

In the quiet moments before the children woke up and Dan came home, she thanked God for sending Tami to her. She'd spent too much time comparing the younger woman's talents to her own and feeling inadequate.

"Forgive my doubt, dear Lord, and make me more accepting of new people and new ideas. And please help Tami's ankle to heal so she can go on to the wonderful career she deserves. Amen."

Feeling refreshed and rejuvenated, Shelley began boxing the cookies she'd been afraid to bake on her own. They were a beautiful tribute to the time Tami had spent with her.

Dan came home a bit disappointed. A Realtor hired him to paint the inside of a house before the absentee owner, one of the summer people, put it on the market. A job, but it would only take him a week or so to do it.

Shelley made his favorite stuffed pork chops to cheer him up, feeding the children first so they could have a calm meal together. The last thing she expected was a visitor while she was clearing the table.

Tami was standing outside on her crutches when Dan answered the door.

"Come on in," he said.

"Please, sit down," Shelley said. "How's your ankle?"

"So-so," Tami said, "but I won't stay long. Since I can't help you anymore, my mom and I are going to visit some relatives in Augusta." She rested on her crutches instead of sitting, a large shopping bag dangling from one hand. "I wanted to say good-bye to Emma and Aiden. I can't tell you how much I've enjoyed getting to know them."

Aiden came out of his room to see who was there, followed by Emma, dragging her favorite teddy bear.

"Hi, guys," Tami greeted the children. "What are you up to?"

She hobbled over to the living room couch, hampered by her long emerald coat, and sat down, leaning her crutches against the end cushion where Aiden immediately went to investigate them.

"You'd better not try to walk with them," Tami said. "You might hurt yourself. Besides, I have something better for you to play with."

She opened the bag and took out a boxed set of three metal cars, Aiden's favorite playthings.

"These are for you because you've been such a nice boy while I was here. And Emma, this is for you. I couldn't resist buying a bear with a chef's jacket."

Aiden thanked her without being prompted and immediately tackled the packaging, freeing the yellow, blue, and red cars in no time. Emma dropped the bear she was carrying and started investigating the new addition to her stuffed animal collection.

"That's so nice of you," Shelley said. "I'm the one who should be giving you a present for all the help you gave me."

"I loved doing it! I'm only sorry I have to leave early." She sounded a bit teary. "You don't know how much I've enjoyed getting to know you and your children. They are so adorable. There's nothing I want more than to have babies of my own one day."

"I'm sure you will," Shelley said, genuinely touched by Tami's words.

"Can I have a hug?" she asked Aiden.

Somewhat to Shelley's surprise, he went over and submitted to a big hug. Tami scooped Emma on her lap and brushed a kiss on the top of her head.

"You're so lucky to have such a wonderful family," Tami said. "And I'm going to leave before I bawl."

"Wait just a minute. I do have something for you."

Shelley hurried into the bedroom where she had a few duplicates of the children's Christmas picture.

"A little souvenir to remember us," she said. "I hope you'll come see us the next time you're in Marble Cove."

"You can be sure I will. Thank you so much!"

Dan helped her out to her car, and Shelley trailed behind for a final good-bye.

"I can't thank you enough for all your help," she said before Tami closed the car door. "You've taught me a lot."

"I'm the one who learned the most. You have a beautiful family, and you manage to take good care of them and run a home business on your own. You're an amazing woman in my book."

Shelley leaned into the car and hugged Tami, then watched her drive away.

The brisk March wind was cool, but inside she was warm with happiness. Tami's visit had brought far more than toys for the children.

While she hurried toward the door Dan was holding open for her, she offered up a silent prayer for all Tami had brought into her life, not the least of which was a new appreciation for how richly she was blessed.

"You look happy," Dan said, putting his arm around her shoulders to warm her. "Aren't you sorry to see Tami leave?"

"Yes, but she gave me a gift too. She taught me to be an even better baker. More importantly, I have the confidence to try new things and expand my business."

"You're an amazing person," Dan said, brushing his lips against her forehead. "I'm the most fortunate man I know."

"Daddy!" Aiden shouted from the hallway. "Come play cars with me."

Dan shrugged and smiled at Shelley.

"A dad's got to do what a dad's got to do."

Shelley's heart swelled with love, and she prayed Tami would some day know the joy of a family of her own.

CHAPTER TWENTY-THREE

Usually rain on the roof of her cottage lulled Diane into a sleepy but contented mood. Today the downpour was beating fiercely against the window in her office, making her glad March was nearly over.

She'd had a good morning, completing some necessary research for her book, although she hadn't actually written anything. Before making her lunch, she wanted to scan a few pages of Jeremiah Thorpe's letters and send them to Beverly's computer. Her friend had more computer skills than she did, and she wondered if was possible Beverly could find a way to enhance the faint, spidery words.

To that end, she'd spread all the pages on a card table set up temporarily in her office. The small room was crowded already, but it seemed helpful to see all the pages at once before deciding which to send to Beverly.

"What do you think, Rocky?" she asked.

He gazed at her with a quizzical expression, as though to say it was up to her.

She took a sip of tea from the mug she'd just prepared, but it was still too hot. Carefully moving aside one of the letter sheets, she put her mug on the table to cool a bit.

Rocky stood up, stretched, and gave her a familiar look.

"You want to go outside?" She wasn't surprised, since his last three trips to the backyard hadn't accomplished anything. As soon as she'd attached his collar to the line she'd had installed for the purpose, he made a beeline for the dry warmth of the kitchen. The weather had been too nasty, even for her explorer-canine.

He stood and wagged his tail in expectation.

"We'll give it one more try," she said, "but this game isn't fun anymore."

Rocky followed her to the door and waited patiently while she retrieved the line that insured he wouldn't run away again. For a dog with a happy home, he still had a rover's instinct. She liked to believe he would've found his way home if kind strangers hadn't taken him in, but she didn't want to test her theory.

While he gingerly explored the yard in a cold, driving rain, she found the old towel she used to dry him off. Diane didn't have long to wait. Her rain-soaked pet made short work of his business and bounded back to the door, standing on his hind legs and scratching to be let inside.

"Doesn't look like we'll be taking a W-A-L-K today," she said, drying his back and face, then lifting each paw to remove the muddy residue.

He stopped to investigate his food and water dishes while she went back to the office.

"Now where was I?" she asked as he bounded into the room behind her. "Yes, I have to choose the best examples to send to Beverly. I guess that means the hardest to make out."

Rocky came up to her, tail wagging for some affection, backing her into the edge of the wiggly old card table. She bumped the edge as she bent to pet him.

"Good boy," she crooned, wishing there was some way to let him know how happy she was to have him back.

She straightened to finish selecting the first page to send.

"Oh my, oh dear!" she said aloud in horror.

Her full mug of tea had slopped over the edge when she bumped the table. She never should've put it there.

Quickly grabbing a handful of tissues from the box beside her computer, she frantically tried to blot up all the spilled tea. Most of the pages had escaped damage, but the one closest to the mug didn't fare as well. Tea had splattered across the writing and soaked portions of the blank space at the bottom of the page.

Working as carefully as possible, she tried to soak up the tea, but she was afraid of smearing the ink. She used up the tissues in the box and hurried to the kitchen to find a soft rag.

What would she say to Reverend Locke when she gave him the letters? There was no good way to explain her carelessness, and he was already angry with the four of them for their expedition to the cemetery.

Close to tears, she sat down beside the damp letter, wondering what else she could do to right her carelessness. The paper was already brown with age, and she could only hope the tea wouldn't stain it too obviously. She piled up some of the dry pages and got up again to bring her desk lamp to the card table, the better to check for damage.

The most incredible thing had happened to the damp paper. A grid of lines appeared on the dampest part of the letter.

She stared for several long moments to be sure she wasn't seeing things. Then, as carefully as possible, she slid a clean sheet of copy paper under the letter and cautiously held it closer to the small lamp bulb. She only dared search the surface for a moment for fear the paper would disintegrate, but there was no question about what had happened. The liquid had brought out fragments of writing and a series of lines that hadn't been there before.

Had Thorpe used some kind of invisible ink to hide what appeared to be a map? Was there something in the tea that brought it out? She was so floored she didn't know what to do.

Her first constructive thought was to call Beverly.

"You won't believe what happened," she said. "I accidentally knocked the table and tea splattered one of Thorpe's pages. And guess what. There's hidden writing!"

"Do you mean the moisture brought out some kind of invisible ink?"

"Something like that, but you've got to come see for yourself," Diane said.

"I'll be right over."

True to her word, Beverly was at Diane's door only minutes later.

"Wow!" her friend said as she closely studied the still-damp area of the letter sheet. "It seems to be a map."

"That's what I think."

"You didn't spill enough tea," Beverly said. "Only part of the map is showing, if that's what it is. I can make out a few letters, possibly place names, but we need to see all of it."

"Do you think we dare?" Diane asked, picking up on her friend's meaning.

"If we don't see it all, we'll always wonder what we missed."

"I'm afraid of getting the whole page wet. What if it disintegrates?" Diane was wringing her hands, anxious but excited at the same time.

"Do you still have the tea?" Beverly was studying the sheet with her nose only inches from the paper.

"Yes, I put it on the kitchen counter."

"Maybe we could gently dab tea on the dry parts to get the whole picture."

"We'd have to be awfully careful," Diane said with a worried frown. "Sooner or later, we have to give the letters back to Old First, whether Reverend Locke wants them or not."

"Do you have some cotton swabs?" Beverly asked, not looking up.

"No, but we could make some. I have cotton balls and toothpicks. Just think—this could be a map to Thorpe's buried treasure!"

"And a way to repair Old First," Beverly said. "You know, the tea stain won't show if the whole page is one color."

"Fortunately, I like my tea weak, but should we use water instead?"

"Let's start with cold water and see whether it brings out the rest of the writing. But don't throw your cold tea away."

Diane gathered the things they needed, including some tweezers to use in cautiously moving the letter. She carefully slid wax paper under the damp page and made tiny little swabs, all the while thinking that Margaret would be horrified at what they were doing to the priceless old letter.

"Do you want to try?" she asked as Beverly pulled a second chair up to the table.

"I don't feel very steady right now."

"First I want just a peek at the reverse side. It seems likely the map was drawn on the back of the letter, and the moisture made it show through." Beverly very cautiously turned the page over.

"You're right! The lines are much more distinct," Diane said.

"Wish me luck," Beverly said, dipping one improvised cotton swab in the dish of water.

"It's like waiting to open a present," Diane said after a few minutes of silence while her friend carefully dabbed tiny bits of water on the dry portions.

"It's working! Look, that's clearly some kind of marking at the end of this line. We have a map, Diane!" Beverly was clearly ecstatic. "Now it remains to be seen whether it's a treasure map. I'm going to take a photo with my cell phone in case it fades when it dries," she added.

"How will we explain the tea stain on the front?" Diane asked, hoping she didn't sound as worried as she felt.

"If this really is a treasure map, no one will ask. After all, none of the sheets are an even color. Even locked away in a trunk, damp air could seep in and stain them in an uneven way."

"Neither of us has lived in Marble Cove long enough to know whether this is a map of the town as it used to be," Diane said.

"You're right. We should have Margaret look at it. She's lived here the longest. And Shelley should come over for a look too. She was with us in the cemetery."

"I'll call them," Diane said.

"I have to take my father to the doctor for a follow-up on his fall, but Mrs. Peabody is making her infamous mashed potato meatloaf for dinner. How about if I duck out on it and come here around five? She likes an early dinner so she can get home for her television programs."

"Fine, I'll see whether the others can meet here then, but first I want the paper to dry. If we have to keep it wet to see it, we have a problem."

★　　★　　★

Shelley had finished baking for the day and was energetically cleaning up when Diane called.

"We've found something exciting," she said. "Can you come over to my house?"

"Now?"

"We were hoping the four of us could meet around five."

"I don't know. I haven't started dinner."

Dan wandered into the kitchen with Emma in his arms.

"Diane wants me to run over to her house for a few minutes," she said, "but I don't have anything planned for dinner."

"No problem," he said. "I'll feed the kids my famous boxed macaroni and cheese. We can order a pizza after they go to bed."

"Are you sure you don't mind?"

"Mind? I love the idea of dinner for two. You deserve a little time outside the house."

"Thanks!" She lifted her face for the kiss he planted on her forehead and put a kiss of her own on her daughter's chubby hand. "I won't stay long."

Shelley was the last to arrive, and Diane immediately ushered her into her office where four chairs were arranged around a card table.

"We waited to see what would happen after the paper dried," Beverly explained after telling Shelley about the accidental discovery of a map. "Fortunately, it's still faintly visible, but I have a photo of it, just in case. Sit here and have a look."

Shelley stared at the aged paper, gradually making out the cause of her friends' excitement.

"It didn't show up until Diane accidentally moistened a small part of the page," Margaret said, her excitement mirroring her friends'.

"It certainly is a map," Shelley said, awed by the discovery. "What's this mark here? It looks like an *X*."

"I thought so at first," Beverly said, "but we think it represents a cross."

"The original Old First Church," Diane said, standing behind Shelley and pointing without touching the paper.

"That's incredible!" Shelley didn't have words to express her wonder. It was like a hand from the past pointing the way, but what was the purpose of the map?

"I brought a copy of a Marble Cove map Allan found online for me," Margaret said, holding out a sheet of paper. "The trouble is, the lines on the sheet don't align with present-day streets."

"We're not even sure the present church is on the exact site of the original one," Beverly said.

"It's pretty close, though," Diane said. "We think this wavy line here indicates the ocean."

"There's nothing to indicate where the cemetery is," Shelley said, moving the lamp closer. "If there was treasure hidden there, don't you think Jeremiah Thorpe would have drawn it on the map?"

"It's a relief to me he didn't," Margaret said. "Allan thought we were loony to traipse through a graveyard at night, and he isn't the least bit superstitious. He just doesn't want me to fall and break something."

"I think we're all glad the cemetery didn't figure in Thorpe's plans," Diane said. "The question is, where does this leave us?"

"If his treasure is buried under a present-day street, we'll never find it," Shelley said.

"Or it could be under the basement of a house," Beverly said.

"Or a public building. Can you see the librarian letting us dig up the floor of the library basement?" Diane asked.

"Most of the basements in town have cement floors now," Margaret said, "although a few may still have dirt floors."

"It doesn't matter," Shelley said in a practical voice. "Not when we don't have a clue where the treasure might be."

"No, but Beverly may be able to use her computer to enhance her photo of the map. She might spot something we've overlooked."

"And if not?" Shelley didn't want to be the skeptic, but buried treasure seemed like the stuff of dreams.

"We won't give up on this," Diane said in a firm voice.

"I agree," Beverly said. "I can't stop thinking of what could be accomplished if we really do find a treasure. Old First could be restored to last another hundred years. Not even Reverend Locke would object to that."

"We have a mission, then," Margaret said with a smile that lit up her face. "If it takes us a year or ten years, we won't give up. Do you agree, Shelley?"

Shelley didn't need to think before she gave her answer.

"I'm with you," she said. "Who knows? We might really discover a treasure. After all, if Jeremiah Thorpe hadn't wanted it to be found, he wouldn't have written the letters and made a map, right?"

Shelley looked around the small room at each of her friends. Their friendship and their penchant for adventure enriched her life, and she thanked the Lord for them. "I do know one thing, though. I can't think of anyone I'd rather go treasure hunting with than the three of you."

About the Authors

Pam Hanson and Barbara Andrews are a daughter-mother writing team. They have had nearly thirty books published together, including several for Guideposts in the series Tales from Grace Chapel Inn. Pam's background is in journalism, and she previously taught at the university level for fifteen years. She and her college professor husband have two sons. Reading is her favorite pastime, and she enjoys being a volunteer youth leader at her church. Pam writes about faith and family at http://pamshanson.blogspot.com. Previous to their partnership, Barbara had twenty-one novels published under her own name. She began her career by writing Sunday school stories and contributing to antiques publications. Currently, she writes a column and articles about collectible postcards. She is the mother of four and the grandmother of eight. Barbara makes her home with Pam and her family in Nebraska.

A Conversation with
Pam Hanson & Barbara Andrews

Q. What elements are needed to make a great story?

A. Characters with depth who are open to growth in their faith are crucial to a great story. Second, compelling story lines that move these characters along on their journeys are necessary. Finally, settings readers themselves would like to inhabit enhance the first two vital elements.

Q. You write as a team. What do you think collaboration brings to a story?

A. Collaboration brings a greater range of experiences to the characters and offers a multigenerational viewpoint. In addition, collaboration makes the creation of a story more fun!

Q. Why is fiction such a good medium to communicate messages of faith?

A. Fiction allows exploration of the kinds of problems real people have and how God can work in their lives.

Fictional characters can mirror the experiences of their real-life counterparts while retaining a wholly fictional existence.

Q. What genres would you say have most influenced your writing?

A. Rather than focusing on a specific genre, we both have been influenced by lifelong habits of reading in many genres.

Q. How much of yourselves end up being in your characters?

A. We both draw on our life experiences, and our characters often approach a problem the same way we would.

BAKING WITH SHELLEY

Date-Nut Bars

2 eggs, separated
1 cup powdered sugar, plus 1 or 2 tablespoons extra
⅔ cup flour
2 teaspoons baking powder
1 teaspoon vanilla
pinch of salt
1 cup cut-up dates
1 cup chopped pecans

Preheat oven to 325 degrees.

Beat the whites of two eggs separately, then combine with the yolks.

Add the remaining ingredients in order. Stir mixture, then spread quite thin in a greased nine-inch-by-thirteen-inch pan. Bake approximately twenty-five minutes. Sprinkle with additional powdered sugar.

FROM THE
GUIDEPOSTS ARCHIVES

This story by Ann-Marie Walker of Mashpee,
Massachusetts, originally appeared in
the July 2004 issue of *Guideposts*.

Twice a year Gary and I took the kids and made the twelve-hundred-mile trip up from Alabama to my native New England to visit my folks, crowding into their cozy little house on Cape Cod. I loved those trips. One year my daughter Michelle gave me a ceramic cottage that looked like one of the saltboxes on the Cape, with cedar trees on either side and a quaint old rowboat out front. "So you can feel close even when you're in Alabama," she said. I gave Michelle a big kiss and a hug in return.

We all got older. I worried about Mom's worsening diabetes. Dad had a heart attack. Suddenly, they were facing a move to a nursing home.

"I can't let that happen," I told Gary.

"Let's move up north and take care of your parents," he said. Our kids were grown by then. It was possible.

We put our things in storage and moved into my parents' basement on Cape Cod, but it wasn't quite the same. The cottage was way too small for the four of us to live in full time.

Gary and I had to find a place of our own. The houses we saw were too expensive or too far from my parents. I tried to take comfort in my favorite Scripture from Jeremiah (29:11, NIV): "For I know the plans I have for you..., plans to prosper you and not to harm you, plans to give you hope and a future." But the longer we looked, the more I wondered what lay ahead for us, for my parents.

One summer day the Realtor showed us a saltbox house down the road from Mom and Dad's. It was lovely. Even better, I had a tremendously warm feeling about it, like those old vacations. I couldn't explain it.

What a relief to finally unpack our things! They'd been in storage so long, it was like seeing them for the very first time. Except when I unwrapped the ceramic cottage my daughter gave me. I turned it over in my hands. The sloping roof, the shutters...it was an exact replica of our new house, right down to the cedars and the quaint rowboat the previous owners had left on the lawn. A hope and a future. It had been there all along.

Read on for a sneak peek of the next exciting book in
Miracles of Marble Cove!

New Horizons
by Anne Marie Rodgers

Finally! Spring was coming. Margaret Hoskins paused to admire Diane Spencer's flowers as she hurried up the pretty brick walkway to her neighbor's home on the last Saturday of March. Diane had been as busy as a squirrel hiding nuts last autumn, planting drifts of spring bulbs around her house and yard to hasten the departure of the first winter she would be spending as a resident of Marble Cove, Maine.

The green tips of daffodils were out of the ground, with a few early varieties daring to show their sunny faces despite the remnants of the last snowstorm still clinging to the area. Striking blue Glory of the Snow blossoms blanketed a bed at one side of the house. Diane must have planted several hundred of the tiny bulbs to produce such a show. Here and there around her borders, clumps of snow crocus in lavenders, purples, yellow, and white had pushed their way through the snow to promise the arrival of warmer weather.

She was going to order some of the more unusual spring bulbs next fall, Margaret promised herself. Like Diane, she loved to putter around in her flower beds, but daffodils and tulips had been the bulk of her spring plantings to date. As she studied the contrast of the bright colors against the gray shingles of Diane's house, her painter's eye automatically sought the best angle for a sketch...there. In front of that holly bush. The glossy dark leaves and red berries stood out against the house, with the daffodils and crocuses ranged in front of them. For anyone truly in love with the season, it would be a feast for the eyes if she could capture it on canvas.

The door of Diane's house opened as Margaret stood lost in thought on the walkway.

"Come on in, Margaret," Shelley Bauer encouraged. "What are you doing?"

"Thinking about painting," Margaret answered her young neighbor. She dragged her mind away from her mental images and entered the house, letting Shelley close the door behind her. "Am I the last one to arrive?"

"You are." Shelley moved back into the living room and resumed her seat on the couch. She wore a rose-colored sweater layered over a turtleneck with navy corduroys, indicating that Margaret's dream of spring was still just that—a dream.

"Yay, you're here. Now we can get started." Diane Spencer rubbed her hands together gleefully, her blue eyes sparkling. Like Shelley, Diane wore corduroys, although hers were a nut-brown and were paired with a butter-yellow sweatshirt, across which was printed, "It takes PROSe to write novels."

After years of working as a journalist, the tall, slim woman had written a novel which was about to be published any day.

Diane had been the driving force behind the formation of the four women's circle of friendship nearly a year ago. "I can't wait to see the results of your search for old maps of Marble Cove. We've got to figure out where that treasure is."

"If there's any treasure at all," Margaret cautioned. She tapped a large envelope she carried. "I did find another old map, and it really doesn't match with the one from Jeremiah Thorpe's letter. On this map, Marble Cove is in the spot where it is today."

Beverly held up the folder she carried. "Here you go. I took the digital photo we snapped of Jeremiah's map and used a program that enhanced the images. I think it came out pretty well."

Diane snatched the thin file and plopped down on the couch beside Beverly, who had just taken a seat. Since Beverly had begun working from home, she'd had more flexible hours, which had allowed her to spend more time with the others than she had when she lived in Augusta and only came to the coast on the weekends to visit her father. It was nice to have her around more. It would be even nicer after the end of April, when she would be leaving her job at the State House and launching her consulting business full time.

As usual, Beverly looked like she'd stepped off the cover of a magazine, clad in a pair of herringbone-patterned wool pants and a button-down shirt visible beneath a soft blue angora cardigan sweater. A silk scarf was looped around her neck in a casually elegant style, and she wore one of the popular charm bead bracelets in blues that matched the sweater.

Surveying the map Diane had extracted from the folder, Shelley frowned. "This still doesn't look familiar at all. Are we sure it's even Marble Cove? Or Maine, for that matter?"

Margaret leaned across the coffee table and laid a second map beside the one in question. "This is a topographical map of the Marble Cove area from maybe fifty years to a century later. Look at the coastline." She pointed, tracing the point where land met water with her index finger. "They match almost exactly. It's got to be Marble Cove."

Beverly and Diane stared at the map, while Shelley craned her neck to see over Diane's shoulder, pointing at the edge of the coastline. "But Marble Cove is over here. This town is…" She stopped and thought for a moment. "This town is in the salt marsh out past the lighthouse."

"There must be some mistake," Beverly said.

Diane nodded. "That land is way too low and wet for buildings."

"Maybe it isn't really Marble Cove," Shelley said. "Maybe this is just an amazing coincidence that the coastlines look the same. I mean, wouldn't it look really different a century later, with erosion and all that?"

"Not necessarily," Diane said. "The beaches might have changed shape, but the bedrock bluffs along much of that area wouldn't have eroded much." She stared down at the map. "No, I think it really is our coast. Although I don't know what to say about the placement of the town."

Margaret had been standing back, watching her friends puzzle over the original map. "You're right," she said to Diane. Stepping forward, she tapped a finger on the lower corner of the paper. She had found a barely visible handwritten note in the bottom corner. Although some of the ink was extremely faded, the words could still be made out.

"Marble Cove, 15 October," Beverly read.

"And look, there's a number one behind it." Shelley leaned forward to squint at the map at the same moment Diane did, and the two bumped heads.

"Ow!" Diane straightened, laughing as she held a hand to her head.

"Sorry!" Shelley rubbed the spot on her own head where they'd collided as she continued to peruse the map. "I can't make out the rest. It's too faded. But it must be the first numeral of the year, don't you think?"

Beverly nodded. "Probably. But even if it's Marble Cove, it's still in the wrong place. And look, the streets are laid out differently, and they don't seem to have the same names. It's hard to tell, but this looks like Pine Street, maybe Maple Street—"

"Someone was stuck on native trees," Margaret said with a smile. "But there's also First and Second Avenues."

"Well, it can't be our Marble Cove," Shelley said, "since the street names don't match."

"Perhaps it isn't exactly ours, but it's located just to the south of the current town, so I suspect there's some reason for it." Diane gave a happy sigh. "Another mystery. I love mysteries."

"And she-e-e-e's *off!*" Margaret clapped her hands sharply, sounding like the commentator at a horse race.

Beverly laughed. "I knew that when I showed this to you three, Diane wouldn't be able to leave it alone until we figured out why there are such discrepancies."

Shelley giggled, and Diane made a face at Beverly. "Inquiring minds..."

"Want to know!" Shelley, Beverly, and Margaret chorused.

In the flurry of laughter that followed the moment, Diane offered her friends some tea and cookies. As Diane went to the kitchen and returned with a tray of treats, Shelley asked Margaret what Allan and Adelaide had been up to.

"Oh, the usual," Margaret replied. "Allan is busy with his woodworking and Adelaide's going to be taking another life skills class down at the community center."

"That's wonderful," Beverly said.

"What, exactly, will she be learning?" Shelley asked.

"Financial tasks mainly. We've realized since you began paying her for babysitting that she can take on more financial responsibility. So this is actually an advanced class where they'll be teaching more complex things about money that we've never taught her, like how to set up and handle savings and checking accounts, how to cash checks, how to budget."

Diane was eyeing her friend speculatively. "Skills she'll need when you're not able to care for her someday." It wasn't a question.

"Yes," Margaret admitted. "Allan and I aren't spring chickens, and Adelaide is probably going to outlive us." She tried to keep her voice level and pragmatic. "We want to prepare her for that eventuality without scaring her."

There was a moment of silence.

Then Shelley said, "I think you're wise to be thinking of the future."

Diane's usually merry countenance was still and somber. "I agree. Who knows what the future holds?"

Beverly merely nodded.

A pang of compassion shot through Margaret. Diane and Beverly both knew what it was like to have one's future change in an instant. Each of them had lost her husband unexpectedly far too young. Quietly, she said, "Yes, we realize that there are a lot of things Adelaide isn't prepared to do on her own. I hope this class will be a start."

There was a long moment of silence.

Then Diane broke the mood. "My, aren't we gloomy all of a sudden? Let's look at these maps again. There's got to be a reason why the town appears in two different locations."

A Note from the Editors

We hope you enjoy Miracles of Marble Cove, created by the Books and Inspirational Media Division of Guideposts, a nonprofit organization that touches millions of lives every day through products and services that inspire, encourage, help you grow in your faith, and celebrate God's love in every aspect of your daily life.

Thank you for making a difference with your purchase of this book, which helps fund our many outreach programs to military personnel, prisons, hospitals, nursing homes, and educational institutions. To learn more, visit GuidepostsFoundation.org.

We also maintain many useful and uplifting online resources. Visit Guideposts.org to read true stories of hope and inspiration, access OurPrayer network, sign up for free newsletters, download free e-books, join our Facebook community, and follow our stimulating blogs.

To learn about other Guideposts publications, including the best-selling devotional *Daily Guideposts*, go to ShopGuideposts .org, call (800) 932-2145, or write to Guideposts, PO Box 5815, Harlan, Iowa 51593.

Sign up for the
Guideposts Fiction Newsletter
and stay up-to-date on the fiction you love!

You'll get sneak peeks of new releases, recommendations from other Guideposts readers, and special offers just for you . . .

And it's FREE!

Just go to Guideposts.org/newsletters today to sign up.

Visit ShopGuideposts.org
or call (800) 932-2145